WHEN IT HITS THE FAN

When It Hits the Fan

VICTORIA COLOTTA

VMC
publishing

Published by VMC Publishing, a division of VMC Art & Design, LLC
P.O. Box 153, Allendale, NJ 07401
info@vmc-artdesign.com

Cover and Interior Design by VMC Art & Design, LLC

Library of Congress Control Number: 2016919449

ISBN: 978-0-9980771-0-9

For all those list makers, organizational junkies, and control freaks. I am and forever will be one of you.

Prologue

Five Years After It Hit The Fan

"DAMN, THESE LIGHTS ARE BRIGHT. IS IT ME OR IS IT hot as balls over here?" I cannot believe that I let Mary talk me into doing this. She continues to explain to me how important it is for people to get to know me. How I need to break the fourth wall or some bullshit like that. What she never seems to understand is that I am embarrassed by some of my actions in the past and I don't want to have to rehash everything for the world to see. My biggest fear is that I will have to lay it all out there. With

Aideen interviewing me, I know that this is more of a possibility. There is no pleading the fifth today. I have the sinking suspicion that I will have to explain why I didn't stand up for myself when I should have, what the reasons are for not thinking I was capable of love, and how I lost who I was for a period of time. Let's not forget that I hate people staring at me. I am better than I used to be, but being in front of a camera to talk about myself is the equivalent to my kryptonite. Yet, here I am, sitting on a TV news set with twenty people staring at me, wearing more make-up on my face that I wore last Halloween, and sweat pooling in my bra. *Glamorous.*

"Don't worry. You will get used to it. Just remember, this is a good thing. You agreed to do one TV interview and I agreed to let you take that vacation instead of starting your next book tour," Mary chimes in from somewhere off stage.

"You let me take a vacation? Mary, I love you and you have been my publicist for over five years, but if you keep saying crap like that I am firing your ass and hiring Margo instead."

"Oh please! You threaten to fire me every other week," she says as she approaches my chair on the set. "Besides, you can't get rid of me. I know where all the bodies are buried." She winks.

This woman will be the death of me. No. She is going to drive me to insanity. Though, some might say I am already there. Lately my sanity is hanging on by a thread with all the projects I have going on. I am waiting for the moment when I go completely batshit crazy and run around Central Park with a cape, screaming *I am Batman.*

Yet no matter how much I complain, Mary Smithson is one of the best publicists/agents out there. She has been there for me from the beginning and I don't know what I would do without her. But…and this is a big BUT. When she wants something, she holds onto it like it is the last pair of Manolos in her size at the sample sale.

She had been hounding me for months about doing this *10 Most Fascinating Women* TV special. I don't see why people want to know anything about me. My life consists of getting up, putting on my go-to writing uniform, throwing my hair in a bun, and then drinking vats of coffee while I type away at my computer.

"You know. One of these days you are going to have to show me these bodies that you are talking about. So, what is the deal? I just sit here and answer some questions?" I ask trying to concentrate on anything but the butterflies in my stomach.

"You will have a thirty- to sixty-minute session with Ms. Walsh where *all* questions must be answered," chimed in a nosy production assistant listening to our conversation.

"Really. *All* questions, huh?" I say with a smirk. Mary just turns and walks stage left in the most dramatic *oh dear lord* head shake I have seen to date.

"Yes. Do you need to see the agreement you signed?" she says while never looking up once from her tablet.

"No. I get it. I just —"

Instantly the set is buzzing with people as Aideen Walsh walks in. To this day, she is still one of the most commanding women I have ever known. From her impeccable appearance, to the way that she walks into a room, Aideen knows how to work it. Today is no different. She is dressed head to toe in designer clothes. Gucci, if my memory of last year's fashion show is correct, and her hair is perfectly styled with not a wisp out of place. *I wonder how much hairspray it took to get it to look like that?* I have always wanted to ask her if her red hair was natural or if it was from a bottle. However, Paula, her daughter, has had the most gorgeous auburn color to her long locks since we were kids, so it is safe to say it is *au naturale*.

As Aideen comes toward me, it seems like forever since I sat in her classroom in college. With a stint on a Bravo TV reality show earning her title of fan favorite, she used her popularity to get a spot on a nightly news program. It may sound crazy that this reality TV darling wanted to be on the news, but people sometimes forget that she was a professor of journalism for over ten years and before that, she spent a brief time as a correspondent in the Gulf War. Now she is the host of *Walsh Takes It On* and her own primetime specials.

"Cami." Aideen hugs me. "Are you ready for this?"

"As ready as I ever will be," I manage to croak out. Suddenly, my mouth is dry and my nerves are kicking into overdrive. *What if I say something stupid? What if I reveal something I didn't want to? What if I say something about my personal life that I don't want people to know? Then he will be dragged into this and...Oh God...what did I agree to? What was I thinking?*

As if she can hear my thoughts, Aideen sits us both down opposite each other. "You are going to be fine. Trust me."

"Famous last words," I say with a snicker as we both sit in quite possibly the most comfortable chairs ever.

"Okay, people. We are set to go in Five. Four. Three. Two. One. ..."

"Tonight we are here with bestselling author Camilla Valentini. Many of you might know her from her debut novel, *Yours, Mine, and the Truth*, but in the years since that release she has penned five other novels. Two of which are set to hit the big screen within the next three years. Welcome, Camilla."

"Thank you for having me. It is truly a great honor to be included in a list with such an amazing group of women."

The first couple of minutes of the interview is very friendly. We talk about growing up in the Upper East Side in New York City, my parents' and grandparents' successes in business, and a little about my education. Then Aideen shifts into news reporter mode as she starts to ask questions about my career.

"Over the past five years you have kept the public at arm's length."

"Yes. I try to compartmentalize the different aspects of my life."

"Some attribute this to you being an eccentric author that embraces your introverted nature. However, others have said that you are an elitist that is looking down on the very people that buy your books. What do you think of that?"

"I'm not looking down at anyone. I love my fans and am appreciative of every single person that has read a book I have written. The truth is that I spend a lot of time by myself or with close friends. I don't share that much because my life is just not that interesting."

"I am sure that others may not see it that way. You are with one of…"

I quickly cut her off. I do not want to make this about who I am dating. "I'm not the type of person that puts everything out there or wants to be seen. It took me a while even to get used to being in the public eye or having people recognize me. It is not something that I'm comfortable with at all, but I deal with it every day. Some days I do better than others. It is why I don't like sharing too much about my personal life on social media. I share what I think people would like to hear about, but most of the time, I just concentrate on work."

"You don't think that people would love to see more of what your day is like?"

"Ha! I am sure that they would, but then they would be shocked. People think I have this super glamorous action-filled life of signings, events, and premieres. If they had a chance to witness my day-to-day, they'd probably be more disappointed than anything else. Most of my day is spent locked in my office staring at a computer screen while typing or talking to myself. Admittingly, I talk to myself a lot when I write and clean, but that is a completely different situation."

"You talk to yourself?"

"Sure. I consider it good conversation with good people."

"People? Is there more than one person in your head at any given time?"

"It depends on the day. When I write a book, the characters are always talking to me. I visualize them interacting with each other. I hear what they have to say and do my best to represent them on the page. Then once I am done, these people I have created leave my head and journey out into the world. They are inevitably a part of me. However, once I am done with the story there are new characters that soon take their place. I realize that I sound crazy right now, but this is the only way I know how to create the worlds and people in my books."

"Is this how you were with your debut novel, *Yours, Mine, and the Truth*?"

"Partially. *Yours, Mine, and the Truth* was started over six years ago. The process was different back then and I was different. Luckily for me, when I sat back down with the work the characters just came at me full force. They became these vivid creatures in my head that needed to get out. I owed it to them to let the world know their story."

"Recently, this book has been optioned to become a movie and there is a lot of buzz around who will be playing the characters and if the screenplay will be true to the novel. It has to be exciting to be in the center of it all, no?"

"It is. I am thrilled that it got optioned, but it is a lot more work than I thought it would be. We started out by having people I didn't know write the screenplay. Unfortunately, it didn't work out as well as I would have hoped. They tried to change key parts of the book to make it more *Hollywood,* and I wasn't comfortable with it at all."

"This was around the time that the studio's emails were hacked which lead to the leak of their emails to you about your response to the script. Some of their executives said that you should *shut up and learn your place.*"

"Yeah. They also called me a brat, whiny, and diva with no real talent. It was harsh to read, but honestly they can call me whatever they want. This is my book and they signed the contract granting me final approval of the screenplay. At the end of the day, this whiny brat got what she wanted."

"So there are no hard feelings with anyone from over there?"

"No. Not that I'm happy with what took place behind closed doors and my back, but these emails came out after everything was already figured out. They had already agreed to bring me and Layla Undine Chisisi in as two of the writers.

"Layla Undine Chisisi?"

"Layla has been my editor since my first book. She feels just as strongly about the outcome as I do. I don't think I could do it without her by my side at the writing table."

"After all of that, is the movie moving forward with your stamp of approval?"

"Things are progressing much more to my liking now. I think that the fans of the book are going to be happy with the way that it will turn out."

"It seems that you are a bit of a control freak when it comes to this part of your life."

"I try not to be, but I think that old habits die hard. Especially when it comes to my words." I laugh, knowing that she has experienced my writer's meltdown once, twice, or fifty times during college. "I like being the one to make the decisions and having the final say. I'm having a difficult time letting go. I know that I have to allow the director and the actors to make it their own, but still…"

As the interview progresses, we touch on a few more questions and topics concerning the movies in the works. Aideen tries to pry out of me some of the casting decisions, but I am happy to say that I did not give anything up. Eventually, she changes topics a bit. "What is it like working with the notorious bad boy of publishing, Patrick Lord?"

"Working with Patrick is a lot of fun. If he believes in you, then there is no stopping how far he will go to help you get where you need to be. The team over at Patty Publishing is an eclectic group, but they have all been amazing. I have been so lucky to have the same designers, editors, and publicity people since the beginning."

"But you do have a history with Patrick Lord, do you not?" Aideen leans forward a bit.

"Yes. We have known each other for a while. In fact, Patrick was the first person to read the book, *Yours, Mine, and the Truth*, after I finished."

"Oh really?"

"Yes. I reconnected with Patrick six years after first meeting him. He was the one who gave me the original manuscript for *Yours, Mine, and the Truth*. I thought I had lost it."

"Reconnected?" Aideen says, trying to see how far she can get me to go with this. It obvious, she wants more personal information and I am afraid to give it to her. *Can I do this?*

"Well, more like we bumped into each other at a restaurant, which started to put us back on each other's radar. He was even there for me at a difficult time in my life."

"This difficult time in your life, that you just mentioned, is it when you lost your home and your job within days of each other?"

Gritting my teeth, I don't want to go there. I don't want to have to explain this.

"Yes. I mean, there are people who have gone through far worse than what I have, but for me, I was truly lost. It started with my apartment going up in flames and soon after completely crumbling because of a small explosion in the neighboring building. I was left without a home and it completely threw me off balance. Then I was fired from my job as a copy editor just days after. The back-to-back incidents left me with no control over what was going to happen next. I had always thought that if you had a plan and worked hard you could achieve anything. But what happened sent me into a complete mental spin and down a path where I had to decide which road to take, as cliché as it sounds."

"Can you tell us more?" Aideen's eyebrow raises.

At that moment, I know that I just opened up a can of worms. I am going to have to tell it all. I am going to have to talk about what happened six years ago and the events that occurred which rocked me to my core. What happened put me in a place that I never thought I would ever find myself in. A place where I was not in charge over what would happen next. No list-making or trips to the Container Store were going to fix it. I was left with my to-go bag and the clothes on my back standing at the front door of my best friend's apartment praying that she would take me in. With a deep breath, I start my story.

"I suppose that if I am going to tell this story, I should start at the beginning…"

Chapter One

Five Years Before It Hit The Fan

I LOVE IT WHEN IT SNOWS IN NEW YORK CITY. Everything is coated in white and there is a quietness that blankets the streets. The moments before the purity turns to grey mounds of yuck and slush piles up to your knees are magical. I sit watching the snowflakes fall outside of my apartment window with a fresh cup of coffee in my hands. It is perfect. I rarely have these breaks in time when I can just breathe. Normally, I am rushing around trying to check things off my to-do list, but today is going to be my day. It is the first Sunday in what feels like forever that I do not have plans with the girls for lunch or have to visit my parents at their Uptown apartment. Not that I hate doing those things, but it is just nice to not be showered and have my baggy sweatpants and grandpa sweater on.

Yet I feel like I should be doing something. I can never relax. My mind is always listing the things that I have to get done or want to organize. Sitting around and doing nothing is torture. I wish I could be one of those people that lounge around all day and binge watch episodes of Gilmore Girls or NCIS. I want to be the girl who can sleep past eight in the morning on a weekend, but I am not. I am a list-making, action-item-loving, highly scheduled New Yorker. I like to get things done.

Today's *must*-do is to write and when I say write, I mean actually add to my word count on the manuscript that will never end. I haven't had much time in the past months. Working at *Exhibition* has kept me so busy with copy editing and fact checking all the articles about the recent load of crazy that has been dumped into politics. Things are really heating up and *Exhibition* wants to be the place online to get all the debate recaps, outlandish antics, and policy out to the public. Which basically means a shit load of work for me and the two other copy editors they have on staff.

When I first started, the online magazine was just a blip on the radar. Not many people even knew about it, but they are growing and getting more popularity each day in part due to the well-publicized fight that our editor-in-chief, Sal Lipman, had with a certain business mogul. It was everywhere and Sal used it to leverage the notoriety of the site. For the first time in his life, people were actually clamoring to see what Sal had to say next. I guess being a brash, rude, and sometimes pervy New Yorker was working for him back then. The other reason why the publication was getting busy is because of my friend Bobby Martinez. He signed on with *Exhibition* two weeks after I started working there to do a weekly celebrity blog, giving his readers exactly what they want: rumors, scandal, and break-ups. Bobby has known the Lipman family since he was in diapers. Sal's son, Joel, and Bobby used to be really good friends, but these days; they don't travel in the same circles.

Personally, I think that Joel's incident back in their senior year of high school with a girl at a party never sat well with Bobby. No one knows all the details, but let's just say that her college was paid for and any formal complaints were dropped. I never quite got why Bobby agreed to work with the magazine, but I think it might have had to do with the number of zeros after an eight written on a napkin when lunching at The Modern last fall with Sal, Joel, and their silent partner, Abel's leggy daughter. For as many morals and rules that Bobby has in life, the all-mighty buck or a short skirt will get him every time.

When I first met the Infamous Bobby Martinez, as he likes to refer to himself, he was protesting the issue that the on-campus cafeteria didn't offer enough vegetarian, vegan, and gluten-free options to the students. I was covering the sit-in and asking different people what they thought about the lack of options and such. I recognized him from one of my journalism classes and bee-lined up to where Bobby was. We had talked in passing and he was great at one-liners. I figured at least he would give me a good sound bite or something that I could quote. But alas, I got nothing on the actual issue at hand. He was trying to hit on one of the activists there and didn't even know what they were protesting. We laughed and when he realized he was going to get nowhere with fruit-and-granola girl, he left to go grab some coffee. Since then, Bobby and I have remained close. When I need a pick-me-up, he takes the girls and I out dancing to show the Latin moves he loves to flaunt. He may not be able to speak fluent Spanish, but the man can dance like a combination of Ricky Martin and Edie "The Salsa Freak" Williams.

After deciding to leave an assistants position in a publishing company, it was Bobby who told me about the posting for a copy editor position at *Exhibition*. He had been checking into the magazine because of their interest in him, and saw the post. I applied and got the job soon after. The job was fine, at first. I would work my nine to five and then have tons of free time for me after hours. I found time to write and hang out on the weekends. Being a copy editor wasn't what I wanted to do with the rest of my life, but it was a good stepping stone in my life plan. However, recently it has been crazy with the volume that the writers and senior staffers have been dumping on my desk. Nine to five has become seven to seven. When I get home, all I want to do is curl up on my bed and crash. Half the time, I don't even have a chance to unwind with a glass of wine. And this is a true travesty.

What pisses me off the most is the other two copy editors have half as much work as I do, but I choose not to complain. I have a carefully laid out five-year plan. First, I shine as a copy editor proving my work ethic. Then I get the promotion to managing editor that Sal and Joel keep hinting at. As slimy as both men are, I hope that they will soon come through on the promises made to me when I was hired. Then a year or so of being a managing editor, I will be promoted to editor-in-chief. From there I will be able to write my ticket. So for all the work I am doing now, it will be worth it...I hope.

In spite of all that keeps circling in my head, I have to stop thinking about plans and work. This is my time to write. I have to push out all the bullshit from the last week and stop running through the list I wrote out on Friday for all the things I need to get done Monday morning. I have to just shut off my brain and focus. *Yeah. Like that actually works.*

Just as I check the ribbon for my 1940s Royal typewriter, make sure that I have a new ream of paper sitting to my right, and go to put my ass in my seat, my phone starts buzzing. *Ugh!* Looking out of the corner of my eye, I see Sophia's face pop up on the screen. My first thought is to not pick up. She can wait. Lord knows she never picks up my phone calls this early, but then I look at the clock. It is eight thirty in the morning on a Sunday. She is never up before noon. What if something is wrong? Something must be wrong. I unlock the phone and ask "What's the matter?"

"Huh?"

"What's the matter? You're never up this early."

"Oh. Can you hold on one sec?" she says as I hear a muffled, "How difficult is it to pour a black cup of coffee. No milk. No sugar. You just have to put the coffee in the cup and close the lid. I mean really it's not like I am asking for a Venti non-fat low foam mocha caramel cappuccino with an extra shot of whatever the hell you put in those sugar-filled…"

"Uh…Soph?"

"Sorry, hon. I just decided to get out of the townhouse and take a walk in the snow. My agent and some buyers were walking around the second-floor studio assessing my latest work. I can't deal with the ass kissers today."

Sophia Pollack was an emerging artist in the New York City art scene. After two of our childhood friends Paula and Jenny featured her at their pop-up gallery ELITE, people started going crazy trying to get her work. She now feels the need to be the contemporary female version of Andy Warhol complete with lavish parties.

Back in our middle-school and high school days, Sophia, Paula, Jenny, and Margo used to be the party girls. Their parents had new wealth and could not wait to make their place in the Upper East Side. From tea parties to crazy costumed galas to your average booze fest, the parties that they all used to attend and drag me to were something to talk about. I never wanted to go, but usually they would show up at my front door and convince my parents I needed to meet new people outside of the public school that I attended. I believe that Margo used to use the phrase, hang out with our people. I still cringe at this.

Let me set the record straight. I was not poor by any stretch of the imagination. I lived in a Park Avenue apartment and never wanted for anything. It was just that my parents believed in not flaunting their wealth. They put their heart, soul, and numerous hours into their business and wanted the world to recognize them for that, not the size of their bank account. They impressed upon me the value of living a normal life filled with public transportation, public schools, and trips to the library instead of the rare book store. I was expected to work hard and then I would be rewarded. My friends lived like they were in an episode of *Gossip Girl*. They had the money, the clothes, and the attitude to go with it. Sure, they excelled in their studies and in other aspects of navigating adolescence, but they wanted to be recognized. Me on the other hand, I wanted to blend in. Not much has changed in the years since.

Today, Sophia lives in a five-story townhouse on Madison Avenue that was left to her after her parents died in a hit and run while walking home from the Metropolitan Museum of Art back when she was in college. After their death, Sophia went into a deep, dark, downward spiral. Her tendency to party and be the life of that party only intensified. She started drinking in excess and surrounded herself with people that only wanted to be near her for what she could give them. Her gatherings became *the* place to be shitfaced and get your next score.

Though Margo, Paula, Jenny, and I never stopped checking in with her, it became difficult to maintain our relationships with her when she was going through all of this. I knew that she would pull herself out of it, but every time I had to hold her hair back over the toilet or search for her in some back room at a club, I wondered when she would eventually hit rock bottom.

Then, one night we all went to her townhouse and the party was still in full swing. We looked all over for her but couldn't figure out where she was. The drunks and druggies she was hanging out with were no help. They were firmly living in la-la land high from whatever they were popping that night. So, Paula tried calling her phone and finally we could make out a ring coming from one of the back rooms. The door was locked, but that was no match for Jenny's Frankenstein boots and years of kickboxing lessons. In two kicks, the door was open and we found her passed out on the floor almost completely undressed. Her then rockstar wannabe boyfriend was setting up a camera in the corner and looked genuinely shocked that we were there. I can only imagine what that douchebag was going to do, but thank God we shut that shit down. If it weren't for Margo holding me back, I think I might have killed him. As it was I managed to knee him in the groin just before she grabbed my arm. He was singing an octave higher when he left and never called Sophia again. It wasn't soon after that that Sophia cleaned up her act and started taking art school more seriously.

"So…what's the matter?"

"Why do you keep asking me that?"

"Because it is before noon on a Sunday and you're actually somewhat functioning in the world."

"Holy crap. It is…damn! It's eight thirty-nine. I never went to sleep last night. I was working on a piece and I guess I didn't even realize what time it was. I knew you'd be up, so I thought I'd give you a call as I froze my ass off while I was walking home from the coffee shop on the corner."

"Well, I'm glad that I'm so predictable that you can rely on me to answer my phone. You know I almost didn't pick up."

"What? Sacré bleu! What could possibly be more

important than answering the phone call of your best friend at the butt-crack of dawn on a Sunday?"

"It's hardly that early, but I was just about to start writing."

"Really? Are you still using that vintage piece of crap instead of the laptop I made you buy last year?"

"It's not a piece of crap. I like the way it makes me feel when I'm writing. Almost as if I'm channeling one of the Greats. I can feel the mojo through the keys."

"I think that Tennessee Williams or Patricia Highsmith wouldn't think any less of you for using the computer."

"You know I'm a stubborn ass and it's all part of my plan."

Sophia's laughter rang through the phone. "Oh yes. The Plan. For a second there, I forgot about the famous Cami's ten-year life plan. What are you, two years into that now at twenty-four?"

"For your information, I'm three years into it. I started when I was twenty-one."

"Okay, Plath. Go forth and write the next Great American Novel."

"Bye, Soph."

"Bye, hon. Love ya!"

And with that I was back to my beloved solitude, sitting at my typewriter ready to take on the world of murder, secrets, and lies.

Chapter Two

"SHE'S COMING AROUND. I THINK HER EYES ARE *starting to respond to the light,"* a man close by states as he is clacking away at his gum.

"I think this one may be gone, man. There isn't much more that we can do."

Not much more? Wait. What is happening?

The voices of two men are clear, but everything around us is mumbled. Why can't I hear anything? Why can't I see anything? Okay. I need to calm down. As I begin the exercises I have used ever since I was a kid with my first panic attack,

I breathe in, hold five seconds, and then breathe out. A few more times of this and I start to make out shapes and forms. Everything is still very blurry, but I am starting to make out where people are standing. Then everything comes into focus as I look up. Staring into the bluest eyes I have ever seen; I realize that this must be one of the two men who were just talking.

"Yeah. You are right. I think this girl isn't going to come back. Sad too. She was what twenty-four?"

I can't believe what I'm hearing. Hello… I am awake you dumbass. Obviously, someone flunked how to tell a dead person from a living person 101. I need to get his attention. I try to speak, but…nothing.

I don't recognize anything around me. It is raining and there is a heavy fog all around. I listen as carefully as I can, but can't make anything else out. Then I notice the flashing lights off to the left. My head will not move because of some sort of restraint, but I manage to shift my eyes to the pulsating lights in the distance. Again, I desperately I try to get up. Nothing. In my head, I rock the gurney to try to get free. I need to be free. My mind is frantically trying to make sense of what is happening. The pain. Oh dear Lord. The shooting pain up my leg to my back is unbearable.

BEEP. BEEP. BEEP.

Suddenly I am standing looking at myself lying strapped down. I see someone in a uniform pull a blanket over my face. How can this be happening? A tall policeman mumbles a curse as my lifeless body is wheeled past him and away from crime scene.

Then I see him. My grandfather standing behind the CAUTION tape. He is frozen watching two men move the body onto their ambulance. As I glide over to where he is, I hear him. He is reciting the Prayer for the Acceptance of Death that I remember from my grandmother's funeral.

I accept from Your hands whatever kind of death it may please You to send me this day (night)

BEEP. BEEP. BEEP.

with all its pains, penalties and sorrows;

BEEP. BEEP. BEEP.

in reparation for all of my sins,

BEEP. BEEP. BEEP. … I jump up and look around as I pat my body with my hands. *I'm okay.* I repeat this to myself as I run into my bedroom to turn off my alarm. *I'm okay.*

With a quick glance in the mirror, I make out the outlines of the typewriter keys on my cheek. *Sexy, Cami.* Then I notice that my bun shifted to one side of my head, and the drool crusted on my chin. *Very sexy.*

I can't believe that I fell asleep while writing…again. I was in such a zone last night that I just couldn't stop. It is rare for my characters to speak to me so freely and have their words so effortlessly go onto the page. It has been an uphill battle with this book, but last night, it was as if all the parts just clicked together. The plot, the character development, and the dialogue merged into about ten thousand useable words. Finally.

With the characters still taking up space in my thoughts, I take a turn into my bathroom to start the shower. I should have enough time before work to get clean, do something with my hair, and put on some makeup so I don't scare small children in the street. Maybe, I can run to my favorite coffee house on the corner of Ninth Street between First and Second Avenue and pick up one of those muffins that could feed a family of four. I need caffeine and carbs for today. It is a Monday after all.

Mondays are always the worst for us grunts at *Exhibition*. We always have our employee recap and assignment meeting at 9:30AM. It wouldn't be horrible, except for the fact that these marathon sessions last about three to four hours. Most of this time is spent listening to Sal talk endlessly about what he did this past weekend and why we need to write a piece on so-and-so who he met at a party. I tend to tune him out about half way through the meeting. My doodling skills have become epic over the past two years.

Once Sal is done with his diatribe, the staff spends the remaining time listening to the pitches, handing out assignments, and trying to shut down Joel's attempt to

start a *Man about Town* column…again. I don't know how many times we can tell him that no one cares who he is screwing this week.

⌘

With my extra-large coffee and giant blueberry muffin in hand, I manage to pull open the heavy metal door and enter into the hallway of our building. Every time I walk down the dark passageway to the elevator, I feel like I am going to be mugged.

As the elevator door opens, I jump in and press four when I hear someone yelling, "Hold the elevator!" And not just any someone. It is Joel. *Oh God. Please don't let me get stuck on the elevator with him alone…again.* Right before the door shuts, Joel squeezes himself through the opening.

"Almost missed it," he says with a wink. "So, Cami. How was your weekend?"

"Good. And yours?" I ask as I bring my coffee up to nose level hoping that the smell of the Arabica beans will make the stench of the cologne become a little less revolting. *Did he bathe in that stuff? Ugh.*

"Oh, you know. This and that. A girl here and a girl there." Then he leans in closer to say, "It could have been you this weekend you know. There is a pillow at my apartment with your name on it."

The lecherous fuck! Not being able to control my gag reflex, I have to turn away.

"Are you alright? Did the coffee go down the wrong pipe?"

"Yeah, I'm fine. I just…" *Ding.* The elevator doors open and I bolt to my desk.

"Oh my Gawd. Were you just stuck on the elevator with Merv the Perv?" my coworker Joann asks.

"Yeah. He slithered his way in just before the door closed. I have to remember to take the stairs."

"Don't be ridiculous. Those stairs are more of a death trap than the elevator. I say a Hail Mary every time I get into that contraption, but I would need to say a rosary before I went up those steps. Four floors." She quickly looks down at her phone. "Look at the time. We better get to the meeting now so we can get a good seat way in the back."

"You make it sound like we are in high school and trying to be the cool kids."

"Sweetie pie, we don't have to try. We are the cool kids," she says as she flings her gray curls over her shoulder.

Chuckling, I grab my tablet and my coffee as we head to the conference room.

ALMOST FIVE HOURS LATER, WE ARE ALL GETTING up to stretch our legs. There isn't one person in this room that isn't eyeing the door or thinking up an escape route. "Alright you all," Sal says, completely oblivious to the obvious stampede that is about to happen. "Why don't I just email you all your assignments? I think this meeting has gone on long enough. And remember, lunch is only a half-hour people. I am not paying you to eat."

"No, you are paying us to listen to you complain about having to share a helicopter to the Hamptons."

Chapter Three

You pretentious ass." Bobby mumbles and walks up next to me.

"Stop it," I smack him on the arm. "These are real world problems."

"How can you say that with a straight face?"

"I'm a gifted actress."

"That you are. We still on for some Salsa this week-end?" He says as he does a little shimmy.

"Sure. I don't see why not. Did you text Margo and Soph about it?"

"I will do it when I get to my desk. How about Paula and Jenny?"

"They are almost done curating a new show. I don't think that either one of them has seen outside of the gallery in a week. I can't see them taking a break now."

"Oh, Camilla," Joel sings as he puts his sweaty hand on my shoulder. "You have a minute?" He glances at Bobby without even addressing him. "I would like to talk to you about something."

A shiver goes down my spine as he walks through the open doorway and down the hall to his desk. There is something so creepy about that man. I still don't ever know how Bobby could have been friends with him, but luckily he has upgraded in the friends department since he met me and Sophia.

"I better get back to the grind. Did you hear that George and Amal are getting a divorce?"

"Really?"

"Not sure. Still have to do the leg work on it, but it makes a good headline. And you know Sal loves a great headline. Talk to you later."

"Bye."

As I make my way back to my desk and sit down in my chair, I look around at the people clacking away at their keyboards. Some are answering emails, others are on Facebook talking to friends, and then there are the few actually working. It was time to get the day officially started. Onto my trusty check list. There are about ten things that I want to get done today. I try to keep a few of them simple and quick so that I enjoy the great feeling when I cross one off. Because there is always that one item I don't want to do. Today's dreaded task…copy editing Joel's latest piece on apartment hunting in the city. It annoys the crap out of me that I am the only one he will allow to edit his work. I know it is my job, but there are other copy editors that would be happy to fix the crap he calls writing.

"I can't. I just can't read this crap anymore. Someone else is going to have to take his pieces," I say to no one and everyone at the same time.

"Another gem from the King of Sleaze?" Janice comes over.

"He actually talks about apartments in the terms of how fuckable they would be if they were women."

"You are shitting me."

"I shit you not," I state as I make the Girl Scout

pledge hand sign. Just then I hear my name being yelled from four rows of desks over.

"Ugh. Talk about the perv now. I don't know how much more of this I can take."

Janice gives that poor-you look that you give to puppies in a shelter and then walks away. Without waiting for my name to pass his lips again, I get up from my chair, smooth out my skirt, and leave the safety of my desk. I give a quick knock on the woodwork beside his door and enter Joel's office.

Most of the spaces in *Exhibition* are professional and any personal touches consist of a potted plant or a family photo. However, Joel's office is the direct opposite. He has vintage pin-up posters on the wall behind where his desk is so that you can't help but stare at the voluptuous women and their breasts when talking to him. Then, on the table between the two leather smoking chairs, there is a stack of what my grandmother would have called *nudie* magazines. Not to mention that his screen saver is the Madonna and Britney Spears kiss from the VMA's circa 2012. This man is a Human Resources nightmare, but because he is Sal's son nothing ever changes. I don't know how many times I should have walked my ass down to HR and put a formal complaint in. It would have been the smart thing to do, but I just knew it wouldn't do anything. Other women have done this and they were fired within a week. I needed this job to help get me to the five-year mark of my plan.

"You are looking good today, Cami. Very good."

"What do you want, Joel?"

"Tsk tsk. Is that any way to treat the man who is about to change your world?"

I raise my eyebrow and let out a huff.

"Don't believe me? Well, how about now?" He slides over two tickets to the annual Film Gala at the MoMA.

"Nice. What does this have to do with me?"

"You are going to go with me."

"No," I say as plainly as I can. "There is no way I am going with you to this event."

"Like I said, you are going to go with me and maybe if you are *nice* then you can finally write an article for the magazine. I know you don't want to be a copy editor for the rest of your life. Now is your chance to get what you want and for me to get something I want."

"So let me get this straight. All I would have to do is get all dolled up in my best little black dress and let you parade me around while I smile and laugh at your inane jokes, right? I assume you would introduce me to all the fabulous people that you and your father always tell us about. It is what the article would be about. You, your family, and your friends making it in the magazine yet again?"

"I think you are getting it." He sits up straight with a bit more enthusiasm than I thought he would.

Apparently grasping the concept of sarcasm is over his head. I bluntly state, "You realize that this is blackmail."

"No. Not blackmail *per se*. Like I said, you would get what you want and maybe even something that you are missing out on," he says with the slimiest smile I have ever seen.

"Are you serious right now?" I start to pace back and forth in front of his desk. "How can I put this so that you will understand it? There isn't a shit's chance in hell that I would go with you to this event."

"Listen to me very carefully." He stands up and places his hands on his desk. "We can do this the easy way or the hard way. Either one works for me. I can just call my father in here and he will *assign* you to go with me."

He walks toward me and puts his hand on my shoulder. I slap it away, but he gets even closer as his eyes move down my dress.

I shiver and pull away. "Do you really think that just because your father can assign me a job that I will go out with you? And then what? What exactly do you think is going to happen?"

"Are you that naive? This is how things work. You go out with me and I can help you get out of the editing pool. Sure, you would be skipping a few steps, but I know that you want to eventually be a staff writer. I know you don't want to be an editor for the rest of your life. How long do you want to be sitting with those people day in and day out?" He steps a little too close, but I am able to slide to the right and get a good distance away from him so that I can think. I just need to think. Then he smiles.

He is smiling at me with the look that most flashers on the subway have right before they open their coats. He is getting off on this. Now I am pissed.

All I see is red. Almost four years of working for a company that I have dedicated my time to and this jackass is standing in front of me telling me the only way that I can get ahead is to date him or worse…sleep with him. Haven't women come further than this? Haven't I? What makes him think that I would actually go through with this? Am I sending off a vibe that I don't know about?

My heart is pounding in my chest and I am starting to have a panic attack. All I can think about it jumping over his desk and punching him in the face. Do what my father always taught me. Hit him in the nose and make him bleed. That will teach him a lesson, but it also might mean that I will get carted out of here in handcuffs. *Calm down, Cami.* I try desperately to regain my composure by breathing in and out. I focus on my plan…my five-year and ten-year plan for my life. You need this job to get to where you want to be down the line. *But is it worth it? Can I walk away and start over again? No. I can do this.* I decide be the bigger person.

"Stop fighting this. You know you want me. Can we just stop dancing this dance that we have been doing for, what, three or four years?" He positions himself so that his arms are circling my waist.

That's it.

"Now you listen to me very carefully. I have put up

with the *accidental* boob grazes, the leering, the disgusting innuendoes, and the blatant disrespect for my ability to do my job all because your father has been promising me a promotion for over three years. I have avoided you any which way I can because you are a repulsive snake who reeks of whatever ten-dollar cologne you are bathing in every morning. Clearly you have no respect for women. I should have said all this sooner and I should have said it to Human Resources, but I didn't. That is on me for not having the balls to have the respect for myself and other women in this office to put you in your place."

"I—"

"Nope. I am not done. In the beginning, I thought that it was just the way you were with new employees or were just too insecure in who you are. I have even tried to convince myself that you are just oblivious to how much of a perv you come off as. However, this," I pick up the tickets and wave them in his face. "This and whatever you think would have come along with it is not going to happen today, tomorrow, or if you suddenly got a lobotomy to become a human being. I will not be blackmailed into dating you or being *nice*."

"Come on, Camilla. Stop using the word blackmail. Such an ugly term. It is a mutually beneficial situation. Everyone wins here. And let's face it. When will someone like you be able to go to an event like this with a guy like me?"

"Hopefully never. And if you touch me again, you will

be on your way to the emergency room for ball retrieval surgery. Though I doubt even a doctor would be able to find them." As I turn on my heels to leave his office I stop, compose myself, and turn again to look at him in the eyes. "Oh, and by the by. I know that you think you and your social circle are the elite of society, but you're not. I received these tickets a month ago from the director of the museum. He is one of my godmother's best friends." A shocked look comes across his face. "You obviously didn't do any background checks into who I am. Big mistake. *Huge.* So, let me give you a little edification. You think that your money and family's name gives you the right to do whatever you want. You are a spoiled brat. I was taught that having money is a privilege that can be taken away by actions or circumstance. I grew up knowing the value of a dollar and that you have to work hard for every penny you earn. Being part of the one percent doesn't give you the right to look down on others or skate by in life. Have some respect for yourself. You have friends because they want you to pay for things. I have friends because we actually like each other. Not to mention that *my* friends and I are all more connected, more socially accepted, and more powerful than you could ever dream of. At best, you are a social climber hanging on desperately to the coattails of your father, praying that no one sees you are a fraud. Outside of *Exhibition*, people don't laugh at you or hate you, because you don't matter to them. They are indifferent and that is the worst thing in *our* world to be."

When the words leave my mouth, I hate myself. Not that it wasn't all true, but I never want to be *that* person. For a moment, there is shock, hurt, and contemplation on his face. This makes me feel even worse for being the mean girl. Of course, I have been known to be a little blunt and too honest, but still, I couldn't control it when all the years of pushed down frustration came to the surface. Having him think that I would prostitute myself out just to get a byline in the magazine infuriates me. Sophia and Margo always told me that you had to shut people down like Joel, but I never do. I just walk away and don't engage. But this time, I hit him where it hurt…his vanity. I had sunk to his level. I feel dirty. Until I hear him say, "I love a woman with fight." All the guilt goes away.

What a prick.

Chapter Four

"I THINK WHAT IS MAKING ME SO ANGRY NOW IS that I actually felt bad for saying those things to him."

"You're too damn nice. Listen to me. You should've said some other things to him. You know the rumors around town about his underperforming gherkin. I would've hit below the belt. Get down to his level a little. If I ever see that—" Sophia was cut off by Margo walking back into the living room with a tray of drinks.

"So have we completely taken off the table going Lorena Bobbitt on his ass?" Margo asks. Her new Fifth Avenue apartment is the backdrop to our bitch session tonight. Never one to shy away from spending Daddy's money, Margo bought this condo and renovated it so that it had an open floor plan. This is the first time we were all getting together since the completion of Chateau de Sweeney.

"I am going to just state this. As the only man in this room, I would like *that* option to be always off the table." Bobby smiles as he grabs the beer bottle from Margo's hand.

"Well, maybe if the men in the world weren't such douchebags we wouldn't have to react in such a manner," Sophia says gesturing for her wine glass to be refilled. "What are you going to do now? Have you made an appointment with HR?"

"No," I hang my head with a little shame.

"Why the hell not?" Bobby demands. "Please don't tell me you think that this is in some way your fault. Cami?"

"I know that he is in the wrong, but I don't want to rock the boat. You know that if I go to HR they'll have to make a formal complaint."

"Exactly," Sophia says.

"And then I'll be fired."

"You don't know that." Bobby says in between swigs of his IPA.

"I don't. What about Sheila, Mary, and Tonya?"

"Who?" he asks.

"See! They were the last three women who went to HR on Joel. They were fired within a week of making the complaint. Sal always uses the excuse of downsizing or some bullshit like that."

"That is the biggest load I've ever heard." Sophia says.

"Yeah, well I just don't know what to do. For now, I am going to work from home. I left a message for Sal and told him that I needed to work from home for the rest of the week because my grandmother needed me."

"Your dead grandmother? The one who is dead. She needed you?" Bobby says with a snicker.

"Shut it." I throw a pillow at his head.

"So let me get this straight. You are going to hide." Sophia says with a knowing look.

"Yeah. For now. I know. I know. But I just couldn't go back there. I have to figure this all out. I want to make sure that what I say is the right thing. I can't get angry again." I take a deep breath and a drink. "When I get back next week, I'll email Ethel and set up a meeting. But if I lose my job—"

"There is no way they are going to fire you. You are the best they have." Bobby cuts me off as he heads over to me to give me a hug.

"I am not looking forward to Monday. To think that I have to see that—"

"Jackass."

"Pervert."

"Immature loser that give all men a bad name," Bobby says as he tries to regain some respect for his gender. "What? I had to try. Fine. How about…jerkwad?"

"I am sticking with douchebag. I think it best represents the subject at hand." I say while I stand up to look out the window.

"And to think that you don't have your own byline with that type of reasoning and eloquence with words," Sophia says.

"Okay, people. I am done talking about this. Let's change the subject to one of my favorite things. Me! What do you all think of my apartment?" Margo swirls around with her arms outstretched.

God bless Margo and her ability to turn everything about her. For once, I was more than happy to enter her little bubble of self-love.

"I can't believe that you're finally finished. What did it take you? Two years?" Paula says as she walks through the door with Jenny carrying enough Chinese food to feed an impoverished nation.

"It has only been six months, for your information."

"Oh. Well then! My mistake. Who wants to eat?"

As we all sit around the table reaching for the cartons of food and passing the chop sticks around, I look around and mentally form a checklist of this motley crew.

✓ **Sophia.** The smart-ass artist who never shies away from telling you like it is. My best friend in the world and the one person I can tell anything to.

✓ **Margo.** The blonde socialite who can blow through money like it is an Olympic sport, but will go balls out for anyone that she cares about.

✓ **Bobby.** *Poor Bobby.* The only man surrounded by a group of women, but I know that he wouldn't have it any other way. He is the one that makes us all laugh when we need it.

✓ **Paula.** She is the rock of the group. With a MBA, she is the most logical and financially driven of all of us. She looks at things in black and white. She is the voice of reason, except where men are concerned. Her choices in boyfriends in the past have not been that great and there was that elopement we are never allowed to talk about.

✓ **Jenny.** The gothic chick that scares most people as she walks down the street with her Herman Munster shoes and spiked collars. Yet, out of all of us, she is the one that is the kindest and has the biggest heart. She is the volunteer of the group and I can't even count how many animal rescue events she has roped us into working at.

I love these people. As cliché as it is to think, they are simply the best people I know. Through graduations, deaths, breakups, and Vegas marriages/annulments, all the ups and downs of my teens and early twenties have been spent with these five. We are the oddest group of people when you see us walking down the street, but here and now, we all just fit.

"Hey. Space cadet. Can you pass the moo shu pork pancakes or are you going to eat them all…again?" Paula says as she snaps me out of my head and back into the conversation.

"I will pass you those, if you pass the wine bottle you have been bogarting over there."

"Well played, my friend. Well played."

Chapter Five

WAKING UP WITH A HANGOVER IS NEVER A FUN thing, but it is a Friday so that makes things a little better. I get up and one of the first things I do is set up the coffee machine to get my much needed caffeine fix. With that all set, I set my coffee mug out and will the pot to boil. It never does, but I always like to think that one day, my supernatural powers will kick in and my powers will actually make the coffee brew quicker. *Man, I have watched way too much* Buffy *and* Charmed *in my life.*

Sitting down at my desk, I place the freshly poured cup of coffee on the coaster and take a quick glance over my to-do list for today. I have been working at home this week because I just can't bear to be at the office. Plus, I get way more work done when I don't have to answer questions from the other copy editors about punctuation or if a word needs a hyphen or not. I have sailed through my work load and even had time to bang out a couple of pages in my manuscript. Looking at the growing pile of papers next to my typewriter just makes me happy. Though I have had several piles over the years, they are all now carefully filed away in boxes on my bookshelf for the day that I am ready for the world to read them. They are just not there yet. *I definitely should retype those on my laptop or at the very least have someone scan them for me.*

Flicking that thought out of my head, I power on my laptop and start checking emails. There are a few with articles that were sent to me from writers at the magazine, a couple of spam, and then one from Human Resources titled "MANDATORY MEETING: MONDAY 9:15AM". *What the hell?*

I check my drafts and see that the email I have been writing and re-writing to Ethel is still in there. I did plan to send it this afternoon, so I have no idea what this could be about. I click on it and read a very succinct message.

Dear Ms. Valentini,

On Monday, I would like you to come to my office on the fifth floor to have a brief meeting at 9:15AM. It is my hope that we can have a civilized discussion about you and your future here at the magazine.

Best,
Ethel

Civilized. Civilized! Is she shitting me right now?

After about the fifth time I read the email, I call Bobby.

"Hey, Cam. What's up?"

"Do you have a minute?"

"Are you okay?"

"Not really. I just got the email from Human Resources and I'm freaking out."

"Can I call you back in five? I'm in a cab heading back up to my apartment. I don't want to be distracted."

"Sure. I wouldn't want a nice set of legs distract you from giving me advice."

"Smart ass. Talk to you in a few."

When I hang up, I open my internet browser, and type in jobs at *Exhibition* magazine. A long list of entries pop up, but only one stands out to me. It is for a copy editor posted yesterday at 4:15PM. As I click on the link, I see that the description is for my job. I cannot believe that this is happening. It basically outlines *everything* that I do. Though I suppose it could be for an addition copy editor. We do need more people and it has been crazy with only three of us for upward of twenty writers in-house, not to mention the freelancers. But then I see it. The one line that sets me into a panic attack. This position will include working as the exclusive copy editor to one of the senior staffers in addition working with other writers on our ever-growing team. *They are replacing me.*

When Bobby's face pops up on my phone's screen, I answer with "Son of a bitch!"

"No one has called me that in a few days. Normally it is when I am sneaking out of woman's apartment… What's going on, Cami?"

"They have my job posted on the site. They are going to fire me. I didn't even have a chance to come forward with my allegations and now I am going to be unemployed. I have never not had a job. Even when I was in high school, I used to work in that small bookstore on Madison Avenue, and in college, I worked at that coffee house part-time. Sure, I was horrible at the job. I never have been *fired*. Never. In the history of my life. I don't know what I am—"

"Cami."

"This cannot be happening. I have a ten-year plan. It is laminated, Bobby. This cannot be—"

"Cami! Stop and breathe. Forget the damn ten-year plan. I am going to come over there and throw that thing out. You don't know that they are firing you. Maybe that dick Sal is finally going to promote you like he keeps promising."

"I don't know about that. You know what happened this week. I basically called his son a douche to his face. There is no way they are going to let this slide."

"Or." Bobby takes a dramatic pause. "Or… Sal has finally realized that you are one of the few people that will stand up to his son and put him in his place. He may surprise you. I have known the man for a long time. Even though he tries to push things to the limits to get the most out of a situation, he does recognize talent. He probably just figures that now is a good time to move you from your position into a different one. Maybe what Joel did pushed him to it. He doesn't want to lose you."

"Or he doesn't want to get sued," I mumble into the phone.

"There is that. I am surprised that Paula didn't mention that last night. But listen. You need to calm down. There is nothing that you can do until Monday, so work on what you have and then take the weekend off. Rip up the to-do list that I know you have hanging on your fridge and take some time to get your mind straight. Take a walk in the park or through the public library. That always calms you down."

"You are right. What would I do without you?"

"Luckily, you don't have to worry about that. Love you, Cam."

"Love you too." With a beep ending the call, I am a little bit calmer. Bobby always has a way of making me step back and look at the whole picture. But, there is something still nagging at me. I can't put my finger on it, but this just doesn't seem like it is going to end well for me. Never the less, I have to get on with the rest of my day. I put the meeting into my phone's calendar and set it with a reminder for fifteen minutes before. Now, I just have to tackle these articles and completely forget about all the bullshit that has happened over the past week. *Yeah, right.*

***

It's 4:55PM. The day flies by as I work my way through about four articles and manage to send out fact check requests for a few others. This was a productive day. I guess being stressed out combined with being on my third pot of coffee equates to getting things done. As I type the last sentence in an email to Janice answering a question if she should be hyphenating a compound modifier or not, I look around my apartment and smile. I love this place. Everything is organized and just the way I want it. I don't know how many trips to the Container Store it took to get it this way or how much bitching I had to listen to from Sophia and Margo as they helped me cart all this stuff into the apartment, but it was worth it. Within these walls I have control over my world. The control I crave and need to stay balanced. I can't say the same when I walk out the door. However, in here, I focus and am able to make decisions to move my life in the right direction. Tonight, one of those decisions is that I need to take some time to relax. As hard as that is for me, I am going to open a bottle of wine and start binge watching *The Gilmore Girls.*

Chapter Six

BANG. BANG. BANG.

Huh? What the hell is that? I open my eyes and look around.

Bang. Bang. Bang.

Someone is at my door, but then I hear footsteps running away down the hallway. When I pick up my phone, my screen displays 3:00AM in bright white numbers. *Who the hell is running around the building banging on doors at this hour?* Then, suddenly the thought of a crazed, knife-wielding murder jumps into my head. I grab the bat laying under my couch that my father got me when I moved into this place and walk slowly to my front door. Looking out the peephole, I see that it is the super's son, Ivan, making all the noise. Undoing the chain lock, I open the door and scan the scene around me. Many of my neighbors are grabbing coats as they shove on their shoes while searching for their pets or grabbing odds and ends as they rush down the stairs.

"Ivan. What is going on?"

"Fire!"

"What? I don't smell anything and there isn't any smoke." I anxiously look around to confirm my statements.

"Fire! Fire! Get out!" The boy starts yelling again as he runs away.

In my life, I have always been afraid of two things: tornados and fire. You would think that it would be getting stabbed on a subway or attacked in the park, but not me. I wasn't frightened of people, though sometimes they do freak me out. The thing I'm most afraid of is mother nature. You can't control mother nature.

I start to feel my heart race as I watch my neighbors give me weak smiles while they rush past me. I need to get the hell out of here. I shove my laptop and tablet into the travel case that is hanging on the coat rack, grab my purse and to-go bag with all my important documents and place them on the couch. Then I run into my bedroom pull on a pair of jeans, a sweater, and my boots. There is no way that I'm going to run out in the middle of the night with my leopard flannel pants and WHAT YOU SEE IS WHAT YOU GET tank top. *This cannot be happening.* One more scan around the room and I remember the jewelry roll that is in my top underwear drawer. It contains the only thing left of my grandmother that I am able to hold in my hands along with a few pieces from my parents and godmother that I got as gifts. I remove the roll from the drawer and place it into my purse.

You can't take everything with you, Cami.

Bang. Bang. Bang. But this time it is different. It is more forceful. Since I never bothered to close my door, there are two firemen standing in the opening just looking at me. Their faces flash from amusement and then to concern as they see that I am examining my apartment for any missed object that I might need.

"You need to leave, ma'am."

Ma'am. Really? Isn't it bad enough that I am being forced out my home at three in the morning, but they have to use the M word?

"Why does everyone keep saying that to me? The alarms aren't even going off. What exactly is going on that is causing this much panic?"

"There is a grease fire in the next building over at the Ukrainian restaurant and we are evacuating the surrounding areas. So please, let's go," one of the firemen says in his most diplomatic tone. Though I am pretty sure that he is ready to throw me over his shoulder and carry me out. *Might not be a bad way to go.*

"Fine. I am going." I throw on my coat and look at my home. Somewhere in the back of my mind, I have the sinking suspicion that I will never see it again. I glance around and spot the signed first edition of Jonathan Franzen's *The Corrections*. Without even thinking I head over to the shelf and take the book. Then the two men escort the family across the hall and myself out of the building.

As soon as I am outside, I am handed off to some more of New York's Finest as they usher us all down the street behind the yellow tape. When I look back, there are flames coming out of the first-story windows where the restaurant used to have tables set up. The glass is all over, but it does not look too bad. Then the ground shakes and the flames grow larger. They begin to engulf the second story of the building and quickly spread to the two buildings on either side. The firefighters are working tirelessly to make sure all of the people and animals are out of the building when I see a group of men running out of the buildings.

Then it happens. There is huge explosion from inside the building and within minutes the building next to ours is crashing down, taking part of my home with it. In this moment, it seems that everything I've worked for and everything I've created for myself within those walls is gone. I have nothing but what I was able to carry out. It's all gone.

How can that be? My neighbors, their families, and I stand there, unable to move as we watch our homes destroyed first by flames, then by water, and eventually becoming rubble in front of our very eyes.

⚬

I am numb. The firemen and police officers lead us to a diner two blocks over so that we are able to re-group and figure out where to go next. *Are they kidding me? I just watched my home cease to exist and they want us to re-group.*

"Here ya go." The waitress with a sympathetic smile hands me a cup of tea.

"Thanks, but do you have anything stronger?" I ask, partly joking and partly hoping that they had some bourbon hidden in the back.

"I wish." And she moves onto the two women sitting behind me.

Assessing my situation, I find that for the first time in my life I don't know what I'm going to do. I always manage to figure things out and create a list of things I to do. It's who I am, but this time, I just can't think. It is almost like I'm outside my body looking at the scene around me. Then I grab my stuff, throw a crumbled ten on the table, and I leave the diner to hail a cab.

The next thing I know, I am standing in front of Sophia's townhouse at five in the morning with everything that I own covered in soot. I don't even need to press the buzzer. The door flings open and she pulls me into her townhouse entrance.

"Oh, Cami. I'm so sorry. Come in. I just saw it on the news. I couldn't tell if that was your building or not. You know that they all look the same to me. Are you okay? I was going to head down there, but they said that they blocked off the surrounding streets. Cami?" Sophia starts to shake me. "Cami?"

"Yeah…I need to sit down."

"No shit. Come on in."

Chapter Seven

"HERE. WHY DON'T YOU DRINK THIS?" SOPHIA hands me a crystal glass with three fingers of bourbon in it.

"Thanks, but it is only six thirty in the morning."

"Well. It is after five o'clock."

"I think that when people say that they mean in the afternoon."

"Oh please! You think I am going to judge you after what you have been through? I am sure that we can make an exception."

I take the glass and head to the window. New York

has always been one of my favorite places. As cheesy as it may seem, the city has always represented endless possibilities. The place that countless people come to make it or to find love or to just escape their pasts. I was born here. Though, some may say that I had a silver spoon in my mouth, don't let my parents hear that. My mom's mother and father immigrated here from Italy with nothing. My grandmother cleaned houses, while my grandfather worked in a factory. Because both came from culinary families back home, they always wanted to open up a shop where they could use those skills. They worked to master English, though I always loved it when they would mix in Italian. They planned and saved their extra money as they worked on their dream of having their own bakery. It wasn't until fifteen years after coming to this county that they were able to invest in a small storefront located where Lincoln Center stands now. They worked tirelessly for years before the bakery took off. People from all over the city used to wait in lines outside every morning and this was before the invention of the croissant-donut. Every day, they got to live their dream and loved every minute of it. Who would have thought that years later, after several relocations throughout the city, their store would become one of the largest family-owned franchises in the country? It was while working at the company's headquarters in Lower Manhattan that my parents met. They fell in love over coffee and a chocolate biscotti, my mother used to joke.

The details of the stories have faded a bit over time, but I can still remember sitting at the dinner table on Sundays listening to the tales of the past. It would start when my grandfather and father had a little too much to drink. They would talk about the past and the words would pour out of them just as quickly as the wine went in.

Listening to my grandparents and my parents made me believe in the power of New York as a young girl. *If you can make it here, you can make it anywhere*, my grandmother used to sing to me. And I believed that. It is what inspired me to start planning out my future at age ten. I knew that if I worked hard enough just like them, I could would make them all proud.

However, now, I look out and it all seems different to me. There is a haze of gray that is washing over the city that wasn't there before. Yesterday, I was happily working in my apartment, drinking wine, and obsessing about the stupid little things. Now, I am homeless with only one pair of shoes to my name. And not only me. There were three buildings of people that are homeless. Where are all my neighbors going to go? I should have stayed to make sure that couple across the hallway had everything they needed for their new baby. Oh God. That poor little baby. And Ms. Petrov. Was she okay? She is in her eighties and I left her there…

"Stop it," Margo says as she enters the room, throwing her purse on the couch and pushing her sunglasses on top of her head. "Stop it right now. I know that you are running through everything you should have done or should have taken with you or about where your neighbors are."

"But—"

"No. Just stop and take care of yourself. You just watched your home crumble to ash. You have to stop and not be *you* for a minute. I know you want to control the situation and your feelings, but you can't. Right now, life has kicked you in the tits." Sophia adds.

"Where do you come up with this stuff?" For the first time in the last few hours I smile. Leave it to Sophia to try to make me laugh. When all else fails in life, I know that my friends will try to make me laugh even in the most inopportune moments. "Life has kicked me in the tits, huh?"

"Oooh! I like it. I'm going to put it on a T-shirt for you." Margo says with all sincerity.

"Oh God." Panic sweeps across my face as it hits me.

"It's not that bad of an idea."

"Oh my God," I repeat as I perch myself on the window sill clutching the glass.

"Honey. It's going to be okay. I promise you. Everything is replaceable and only you would have a to-go bag ready for an emergency. You didn't lose anything important. Right?" Margo releases me from her hug as she stares into my eyes. "Cam. What? Why are you completely pale? Cam. You are scaring me."

"With everything that happened, I forgot to take the

manuscripts. I took that stupid first edition Franzen, but I didn't think to take *my* books."

"Oh shit," Sophia yells as she stomps her way into the living room from her kitchen. "You and that God damn typewriter. I told you that you should stop using it and act like you are part of this century. If you had, you would have had everything in the Cloud."

"I don't think this is the time to start yelling at her, Soph," Margo says out of the side of her mouth.

"No. She is absolutely right. I lost over five years of work because of what? Because I thought that I was the next female Hemingway and needed to have the same experience as the great American writers? I am such an idiot." I chug the rest of my drink and hold it up to get more.

"You're not an idiot. You are a pain in the ass, a control freak, and more stubborn than me, but not an idiot. Maybe it was supposed to happen this way?"

"Are you serious right now, Soph? You are going to give me that 'everything happens for a reason' crap on me now?"

"Shut it and listen. If you had the instinct to take your grandmother's jewelry and the book your father gave you for your birthday, but didn't take your *life's work* as you are calling it, don't you think that something is up with that? I sure as hell would grab a couple of paintings if this place went up in flames. Or at the very least, my sketch books."

The silence in the room forces me to think. *Maybe*

she's right. Why didn't I get at least one box with a manuscript in it? This question keeps circling around my head as I take another sip of the brown liquid that burns while going down but at this moment is the only thing calming my nerves.

Just then, Bobby, Paula, and Jenny come barreling through the door and bee-lining right at me. As they smoosh me between their bodies, I finally gasp out, "Can't breathe. You are squeezing me."

"Sorry, but when a friend almost dies, I get to hug her to death," Jenny says as they all pull away.

"Are you okay?" Paula looks me up and down, checking for any sign of bruises or cuts.

"I am fine. Well, not fine, but I wasn't hurt. The firemen got us out before the real damage happened to the buildings."

"Good. I would have hated to visit you in the hospital. You know those places freak me out," Bobby says as he pats me on the back and goes over to the tray of food that Sophia just put out.

"What are you going to do now?" Jenny asks while filling up a cup of coffee.

"I don't know."

"You had renter's insurance, right?" Paula, always the pragmatist, would of course be the person to ask that now.

"Yes. I will have to call them next week."

"And you are thinking about staying…where? Your parents' place? I am sure that you can stay with them."

Paula has already moved me back in with parents so that I can save money and get a new place. She never liked my place on the Lower East Side and has said so more times than I could count. It seemed silly to her that I would make the choice to live on my salary instead of just touching the inheritance from my grandmother. I did dip into it a little to start me off so that I wouldn't have to live with any roommates, but I felt it was important to keep most of that money set aside, just in case.

"Actually, I can't. They finally took that trip to France and Italy that they have been talking about and will not be back for a month or so. They sublet their apartment to a family friend and I have no intentions of living with a single dad and his three kids. Though I do think that Dougie would offer me a room if I told him what happened."

"So a hotel?" Bobby asks.

"I guess so."

"Have the smoke fumes and ash gone to directly to your brain?" Sophia questions. "You will stay here with me. I have three extra bedrooms for you to choose from. It will be like college again. Oh, the fun we will have!" She slaps her hands together.

"Yeah…just like college," Margo says under her breath.

"Excuse me, *Missy*. But shall I remind you that not one but four of you stayed in this very townhouse during your college years."

"That is true, but do you remember what it was like having roommates?" Paula directs the question to Sophia who seems to be oblivious to the fact that we all almost killed each other the last time the four of us had lived under this very roof.

"You know. The ones that don't sneak out at the wee hours of the morning," Jenny mumbles just before a pillow is thrown squarely at her head.

"Pillow fight!" Bobby screams. "I have been waiting for this moment my whole life."

With that all five of us grab a pillow and, almost in unison, throw them at him.

❧

"So, how are you really?" Sophia sits at the edge of the bed in the guest room that I picked.

"You want the truth or what you want to hear?"

"It is before ten o'clock in the morning and I have a decent buzz from all the bourbon we drank, so let's go with the truth this time around."

"I don't know. I am sort of heartbroken. I made that place my home. I knew it wouldn't be forever, but I never thought it would go up in flames." I close the curtains. Suddenly the sunlight is just too much for my eyes. "It was great that you all tried to distract me and make light of everything, but I just feel a bit lost. I am numb."

"That is understandable, right? When everything happened with my parents, there were months that I just walked around feeling nothing. I was sad and I cried a lot, but most of the time it was like I was in a fog."

"That is exactly how I feel." I slap my hands over my mouth. "Oh God! I cannot believe that I said that. I am not comparing losing my apartment to your parents. You went through a true tragedy and I just lost my underwear and shoes."

With a chuckle Sophia looks me right in the eyes and says, "I know what you are saying, so for once, stop acting like yourself."

"Why do people keep telling me that?"

"Because we know you. We know how your crazy, twisted little brain works. And for now, you need to not act like you normally do. You can't control what happened. It wasn't your fault. You need to take a minute to process and grieve for what you lost."

"And then I will start to…what?"

"You will get back to your control freak self, trying to plan your way out of dealing with any residual emotions. I am sure that a list is already forming in your head."

"I just feel like my whole world got shifted off balance."

"You lost your home. That sucks, but you are not off track. You just have been relocated. And may I add what an upgrade you have got? Look at this place."

Shaking my head, I can't help but realize how lucky I actually am. "What am I going to do with you, Soph?"

"Nothing, but you could make me dinner tonight. I haven't had a home-cooked meal in…when was the last time you were over here to cook?"

"Don't you have plans? It is a Saturday night. I am sure that someone out there would like to kiss your ass both figuratively and literally."

"Wish that it was the truth, but you know what it is like out there. The men are all looking for either a wife or just a one-night thing. And I am not desperate enough to go the whole lesbian route."

"Good to know."

"Anyway." She waves her hand in dismissal as she starts to exit the room. "So how about you relax for a bit while I go paint? Then we can run out to Whole Foods and pick up what we need for the perfect night in."

"Sounds like a plan. I should check my emails and then give my parents a call. They are going to want to know what is happening. I just hate to ruin their trip."

"Please! Your mother will be so happy that you are back on the Upper East Side; she will gloss over the horrible way it happened. Don't you remember when you moved in? She made a big deal about risking her life just to see her daughter. I think she even started to carry wasp spray with her *just in case*. Call your parents and let them know where you are. Because if they find out from someone else, you know that it will be a shit storm of guilt."

For the first time since this morning I am actually alone. I shut the door and slide down the front of the bed to the floor. I can't believe this happened. *What am I going to do?* And with that, I get up and grab the sketchbook and pencil sitting on the dresser. I am going to do what I do best.

TO DO:

1. Call insurance company - renter's insurance.
2. Call Aunt JoJo - start apartment hunt.
3. Shopping - Clothes. Shoes. Underwear.
4. Get more bourbon.

I tap the pencil on the paper and add one more item.

5. Get writing again — Use the freakn' laptop!

There. This is a good place to start. Sophia was right, I did have a list formulating in my head. I hate it when she is right.

I am tired. I look around at the neat pile of my remaining possession and take a moment. It just seems surreal to me. I am, for a lack of a better word, homeless. Shaking my head, I place the list on the night table and climb into the oversized bed. The only thought that comes into my head is *this isn't my bed*. Yet, when my head finally rests, I feel myself getting pulled into sleep.

Chapter Eight

SMOKE FILLS MY LUNGS AS I WALK DOWN AN *endless hallway. All that I am able to see is a faint outline of door. Yet, no matter how many steps I take toward it, it is never in reach. I try to lean up against the wall, but jump away as my arm is burnt from the heat radiating off of it.*

Fire. Feeling the flames against my skin as I get hotter and hotter. Yet, I am not burning. The intensity is growing as the ground under my bare feet starts to shake.

Just then I notice the cracks in the wall getting larger as the building begins to splinter. I look around for anything to save me, but there is nothing to hold onto. Just then the floor suddenly opens up into a giant sink hole.

Quickly, I try to grab onto anything when I see a door knob. Instinctively I reach for it and attempt to turn it. Nothing. It doesn't budge until it starts melting in my hand. The mercury-like substance oozes its way through my fingers.

Then another rumble and I completely lose my footing. I am falling down a dark hole. I keep falling…falling…

"Cami. Come on. Get up." Sophia has both of her hands on my shoulders and is shaking me. "It is just a dream."

"Uhhhh…What?" I dart up from the bed, grabbing my glasses from the night table. "Where? Huh?" It all sinks in and I plop myself back onto the bed. Not that I need to remind myself, but the events of the past day start replying in my head. The evacuation of my building. The fire. Everything is gone.

"Get your ass up. I have let you sleep, but its Sunday. You need to get up and come out to lunch with us all. It will be good for you. I promise."

"Really? Do I have to?" I hate how pouty that came out, but I really don't want to go anywhere.

"Yes. Stop being a butthead. Get. Up." She takes both of my arms and drags my limp body across the bed. For such a petite person, she is surprisingly strong. It must be all those years of lugging art supplies and canvases all over the city.

"Ow! I think you just pulled my arm out of its socket."

"Well, that is what you get," she says with a proud smirk on her face.

"Alright. Do you have something I can wear?"

"Do I ever!"

"Oh brother. What have I just done…" Ever since we were in high school, Sophia has wanted to help me develop my style. It has taken all my strength to resist her up until this moment, but what choice do I really have. I could wear my clothes from yesterday, but they still smell of smoke and have ash on them. I have no other options. I think I just opened the Pandora's box of fashion. *Someone save me.*

Two hours and several costume changes later, Sophia and I walk into a new restaurant that has been getting a lot of buzz lately. It was opened about a year ago by the chef who was a runner-up from one of the first seasons of *Top Chef*. Since Margo is the publicist for the chef, we have been able to get a table. Otherwise, I have a feeling that we would be lunching elsewhere.

When I pass through the red wooden door, I instantly love it. There's a homey vibe to it, with comfy chairs, rustic tables, and pops of color all around. They even have fresh cut flowers on all the tables in Depression glass vases.

"Here is hoping that the food is as good as this place looks," I whisper into Sophia's ear.

"Oh it is," a male voice says behind me. My body responds to the deep sound of his voice because it is not just any male voice. It is *his*. The British accent still makes me go weak at the knees or at least wobble in Sophia's stilettos.

"Patrick!" Sophia turns around and gives him a tight hug. "You having lunch here too?"

"Actually, I was just leaving. The food was divine. You must have the pork tenderloin with balsamic plum reduction. I would stick around, but I…" his sentence trails off as he becomes distracted. Suddenly he is tapping his pockets, trying to find either his phone or wallet.

But then, as if on cue, a bubbly young waitress comes running over with her boobs almost bouncing out of her low-cut top to give him the phone. "Here you go, Mr. Lord. If you need anything else." She smiles coyly as she hands him back his phone along with a slip of paper with what anyone would assume is her phone number.

"Really? You have got to be kidding me." Everyone turns and looks directly at me including the waitress. "Oh crap. I thought I just said that in my head."

"And you are?" Patrick walks right in front of me so that he is inches from my face.

"Camilla Valentini. And you are Patrick Lord."

"I love it when a woman knows who I am. I know you. Don't I?" he looks at me as if searching for the place that we have met. "Don't tell me…you were at the Hamptons Black and White party this summer. No…No…that club opening last weekend in Tribeca!"

"No on both accounts. Actually." I pause and see that there is a small glimmer of recognition in his eyes. "I used to be your father's assistant after I got out of college about six years ago."

"Huh. I could have sworn that we met somewhere else." This is a game to him. There is no way that he is going to let on that he knows who I am. "Anyway, I am sorry to hear that you've had the *pleasure* of working for Dear Old Dad. I hope he wasn't…well…him."

"It was an interesting experience. I only lasted six months."

"At least you got out. I suppose that we could have bumped into one another while I was visiting your former employer."

Looking at him standing in his perfectly tailored suit staring right back at me, I start to question the connection that I thought we once had. Patrick has had his fair share of women over the years. I was just one of many. Hundreds if Bobby and the tabloids are right. Maybe I am making myself more important to him than I actually was. I could have been just another girl he shagged in his office. He may not even recognize me. The last time he saw me I had bleached my hair so that it was almost white and chopped it off into one of those severe bobs. I never wore my glasses and there wasn't a day that went by that I didn't have my signature red lips. It is a far cry from the wavy long reddish brown hair, dark-framed glasses, and lip gloss I am sporting today. When I look back, I cringe. Who was I trying to impress? The answer... everyone. I don't even recognize myself when Sophia pulls out pictures from back then. I am going to have to put that in the *what the hell was I thinking* column along with most of my grunge years and the baby doll dress with combat boots phase.

"I think that you may have seen her at my openings too." Sophia winks. She knows all when it comes to my life and the Patrick months are some of her favorites. "Or maybe you ran into Camilla over at the *Exhibition* offices? She is a copy editor there."

"That rag! Is that horrible bender Joel still running around pretending to have any writing ability while he runs Daddy's magazine into the ground?"

Trying to hold back my laughter, I manage to get out, "Yup. Still there."

"Miss." A leggy brunette wearing what I can only imagine is a T-shirt she shrunk in the dryer and put a belt on says to Sophia, "Your table is ready."

"Thank you. We will be right over." Sophia gives Patrick double kiss goodbye.

Then he turns his attention toward me. "It was nice to meet you, Cami. I would say, I could call you, but sadly I don't have your number."

"Seriously. That is the best you can come up with?

The infamous player of New York City and all you have is you wish you could call me but you don't have my phone number. Sad, I held you in higher esteem than that. If you really try, I think that you can do better. See you around, *Patty*." If for some reason he didn't remember me before, he will now.

"No one has called me that since…" Patrick Lord knows exactly who the girl standing in front of him is. I can see recognition in his eyes. He looks me up and down. Then, just as he is about to say something, I turn to walk away knowing that he is smiling and shaking his head like he used to.

Chapter Nine

WE MAKE OUR WAY TO THE TABLE IN THE CENTER of the restaurant and I sit down across from Sophia. As usual, we are the first to arrive. Luckily for me, Sophia's phone rings and she is chatting away with her art dealer. While I look at the menu, my mind cannot stay focused on the entree list that is in front of me. My brain keeps going back to when I first was out of school and obsessed about getting a job. Then there was the weirdest interview of my life, a job at LORD Publications, and Patrick. Oh, Patrick. That man is still in my flashback reel of men. He knows how to leave an impression.

The summer after college was spent searching the classifieds in the *Times*, printing resumes, and making countless trips to the mailbox at the end of my street. I had gone on eleven interviews, but none that were going to lead to anything. Since I was only applying to places that could help me get to where I wanted to be in ten years, the pool of potential jobs was limited. I had a plan. Every day I would sit and stare at the printed sheet pinned to my cork board.

Cami's Ten-Year Plan

1. Graduate college with a degree in Liberal Arts and a minor in journalism.
2. Get a foot in the door! Take a job at a top ranked publishing house or popular magazine.
3. Move to the editorial department (if not already there).
4. For the next six years, work towards advancement and promotions.
5. Reach goal of being one of the youngest Editor-in-Chief.
6. Make connections with all the Who's Who of publishing.
7. Write (finish) a novel.

8. Get an agent and publish book with one of
    the top five publishing houses.
9. Hit the bestseller lists.
10. Move to the Hamptons and continue a
    career as a novelist.

This list pushed me to keep searching, but it was my twelfth interview that nearly broke my idealized vision of the future.

Then in August, I was starting to get itchy about not having a job. Sophia, Paula, and Bobby were all employed and doing what they loved to do. Margo was on an endless hunt for the perfect apartment for Daddy to buy as a graduation present. Jenny was backpacking across Europe in search of every unknown artist she could find.

After spending four years living with Sophia and the girls, I decided to move back with my parents for a little bit to regain focus. So, there I was, sitting in my childhood room with lists, stacks of resumes, and a serious nail-biting problem developing. When the phone rang, I jumped to answer it.

"Miss Valentini?" A nasal-sounding woman questioned.

"Yes." I was fully prepared for the onslaught of a telemarketing sales pitch that had been flooding my phone.

"This is Natalie from *Opinion*. You sent in your resume for the junior editor position and we would like to set up an interview with you."

I remembered the classified ad. It was for a small

newspaper located down in Dumbo, Brooklyn. It was certainly not my first choice, but I was running out of options. The newspaper was a free publication earning revenue from advertising. They were a bit more New Age than I would have liked, but the alternative publication had a niche readership that spanned across many generations and backgrounds. The posting said that they were looking for a junior editor with a fresh approach, attention to detail, and a willingness to learn.

"Really? That is great. When were you thinking?" Trying desperately not to sound too available or interested.

"Tomorrow at three. Would that work?"

"Sure, I believe I can make that happen."

"Great. Just so you know, the elevator is broken so you have to walk up the steps to the sixth floor. Someone will be around and you can just let them know why you are there."

"Thank you. I will see you then." Walking up six flights of steps was not going to be fun, but it was an actual editing position.

The next day, it took a little over an hour to get to the building, but at least I was able to refresh my knowledge about the newspaper. As I started to run through the facts on the printout that I made, I realized that this trek to Brooklyn every day was going be quite the commute. At least I would be able to catch up on my reading.

When I got off the train, I was hit with the oppressive heat that only New York in the summer can give you. It was ninety-seven degrees out and I was sweating like a whore in church. Taking out the map that I had printed out, I made a left and started walking. By the time I got to the street where the building was located, I was a mess. My feet were killing me and my hair looked like I just got out of the shower. Thank God there was a Starbucks on the corner. I went in bought an iced tea and locked myself in the bathroom to assess the damage. I had fifteen minutes until the interview. I could make this work.

By the time I made it up to the sixth floor, I was at least remotely presentable. Looking around, I saw an elderly man in his eighties sitting at a desk in the front reading.

"Excuse me. I am Camilla Valentini. I am here for an interview?" The last bit came out as a question even though it was a statement in my head.

The man looked up, smiled and stuck out his hand to shake mine. "I am Marco Brodery, the editor-in-chief. It is a pleasure to meet you. Let's go back into the conference room."

While following him through the endless rows of desks, I tried to see what I would be getting myself into if I worked there. To say that there was an eclectic group would be an understatement. There was an array of old hippies that time had forgotten, a group of thirty-year-old tattooed men, and a small collective of younger twenty-somethings staring at their computer screens like their lives depended on it. But who was I to judge? They were the ones with a job.

Marco gestured for me to sit in the beanbag chair opposite the one he just plopped himself in. As gracefully as I could, I lowered myself to the floor.

"So, Camilla. Do you have a resume?"

"Of course." I quickly handed him the sheet with my initials embossed on the upper right corner.

"You were the head of your college newspaper, graduated Cum Laude, and it appears that you have interned with an interesting range of publications. Any reason why someone hasn't snatched you up yet?"

"Honestly, I don't know. I guess I haven't found the right fit yet."

"Finding the right people is very important to us." He eyed a woman in a flowing caftan as he made a waving gesture for her to come in. "Evangeline!"

The older woman turned and came into the conference room. "Hey. And who do we have here?"

"I am Camilla Valentini." I said as I tried to get my ass out of the damn chair.

"Please don't get up. I will sit. May I?"

"Please," Marco stated. "As I was saying, Camilla, it is very important to us that we find the right fit for our little newspaper, so would you mind if Evangeline reads your palm?"

"Read my palm?"

"Yes, dear. It isn't painful. Just a quick look," Evangeline said in the most melodic tone.

"Um…" I looked around to see if this was a joke

that Bobby and Sophia was playing on me. "Sure. Why not?"

The woman took my hand and ran her fingers over my palm. For several moments there was silence. I thought she fell asleep, but then she started to speak.

"You have been very privileged in your youth and have chosen to live a structured life. Your plans are careful and neat, much like your mind."

Okay. This has to be a joke. Am I being punked?

She grabbed my hand and held on tighter as she continued. "Events will shake you to your core. Decisions will be made for you. Trust that all will be revealed in time. Your path is uncertain, but your choices will define who you will become. At one point, you will lose your footing in a distracted moment. Fear not. This will allow you to find your mainstay. It is important that during difficult times you open your heart. You do not give love freely. I see pain from your past that has caused you to keep lovers at arm's length. I advise you to choose to take a leap of faith. Though it could seal your fate, I only see positive energy around this."

For a moment, I sat and stared at the woman in front of me. In an instant, I thought I saw her eyes almost flicker with sparkles of gold before they went back to brown.

"I see that something you thought was lost will come back to you. Pay attention to this. There are voices other than your own that you need to listen to. Find out their story. I cannot stress enough, you must open yourself to change and uncertainty before you will see the path you are meant to be on."

"Um…thank you?" I didn't know what else to say.

Evangeline looks at me once more to say, "This is not the job for you."

With that my interview was over. I was ushered to the front of the offices and thanked for my time. Before I knew it, I was back on the subway to Manhattan wondering what the hell just happened. The woman's words kept repeating in my head. Whatever Evangeline the Magnificent said was just a bunch of crap. It had to be. Yet, there was still something bothering me about what she said.

The pain of my past was really hitting me. Could she really know? Was it public knowledge what happened to Joseph or maybe they just did research on their candidates? I don't remember anything but an obituary being in the papers. I certainly wasn't mentioned.

Joseph Bradford was the first man I fell in love with. We met at orientation in college and by senior year we were inseparable. Then, sometime after Spring Break, Joe started to act different. Everyone thought it was just nerves about entering the real world and getting a job, but I know that there was something else. He was pulling back from all of us emotionally, and would get violently angry for the smallest things. The man that used to eat hamburgers and fries at almost every meal was living on a diet of coffee and cigarettes. His weight loss was rapid and startling. Yet that wasn't the worst part. The mood swings scared me. I would spend nights with him trying to calm him down, but he just pushed me away. One night, three weeks before we graduated college, we had a huge fight. He smacked me in the face, but then instantly started apologizing. I decided that I couldn't take it anymore. I told him it was over. It was the last time I saw him. Four days later, his roommate found him unresponsive in his bed. He died at the hospital two hours after he was admitted. It was a heroin overdose. After that, I cut myself off to the possibility of ever getting hurt like that. I convinced myself that I didn't need love. Sometimes, I believed that I didn't deserve it.

I snapped out of my trip down memory lane when I heard the conductor mumble my stop. Feeling defeated and running out of options, I was happy to see a text saying Jenny was back early from her European excursion. We were all hanging out at Paula's house for a night in with pizza and wine. It was the perfect distraction. And maybe Paula's mom, Aideen, would be there. Aideen Walsh was not only one of the best writers that I personally knew, but she was a teacher and my advisor from college. It was just a bonus that Paula got to call her mom.

That night, I stopped by the liquor store and picked up a couple of red before I went to Paula's new apartment. It was a graduation gift from her real estate developer father. The building was a classic structure, but the inside has been completely gutted and turned into modern full-floor living space. Pressing the PH button in the elevator, I thought about the history that was eradicated from the building. Very little was left of the pre-war details and it was a shame. I would never say so to Paula or her dad, but I loved the classic architecture much more than the sterility of the modern concrete spaces that were being built these days.

Yet, as the elevator doors opened directly into Paula's apartment, I was surprised by the warmth. "This place is swanky."

"Thanks. It is a bit much if you ask me, but you know my dad. You are here early. I am shocked."

"Very funny. I wanted to make sure that I had enough time to get some vino." I held up the bags with the bottles clinking.

"You know I have wine. I don't know why you insist on bringing more."

"Because your wine is that sweet crap. I can't drink that stuff."

"She has Champs too," Aideen chimed in as she emerged from the kitchen.

"Aideen!" I nearly leaped over the ottoman to give her a hug. "I was hoping to see you."

"Uh oh. What is going on?"

"I just had the weirdest interview at the *Opinion*. It has been the twelfth one that has ended with no job offer. What am I doing wrong?" I pouted as I worked my way over to the wine opener.

"First of all. The *Opinion*. Are you serious? They are all New Age, crystal-loving—"

"Mom!"

"Sorry. They are not a publication where you should be working."

"That is what Evangeline told me after she read my palm"

"A Palm reader at an interview. Seriously?" Paula raised her eyebrow. "I'm so going to have to hear about this."

"I have it!" Aideen looked up from her phone. "Theo is looking for an assistant."

"An assistant?"

"Don't look at me like that. This is the assistant position for Theo Maclaren Lord of LORD Publications. The last girl who had the job quit or was fired or something like that. He was left in the lurch and is desperately looking for someone to fill the position."

"I don't know. Being someone's assistant wasn't really the plan."

"Camilla. Listen to me very clearly. There are thirty girls who have already applied for this job from Ivy League colleges because working as Theo's assistant can help you write your own way into any one of his companies."

"Mom. This isn't like the *Devil Wears Prada*. You don't have to be so dramatic about it." Paula said as she walked into the kitchen.

"Still. I am texting Theo personally and giving him

your information. We have worked together a couple of times and have a mutual admiration for one another." Aideen said. I could tell she was on a mission.

"Ewwww. Mom! Seriously," Paula said. "I don't want to know about your admiration for anyone. It is bad enough Dad can't keep it in his pants with anything that isn't between the ages of twenty-one and twenty-eight."

"Between twenty-one and twenty-eight?" I ask, dying to know the answer to this one.

"Yeah. He thinks that twenty-one is good because they can legally drink and twenty-eight is just far enough from thirty. Or as he likes to call it The Marrying Age." Paula said right before she took a shot of something. This topic was obviously making her uncomfortable.

"That sounds like your father. Well, prepare to hear from LORD's Human Resources department soon. Theo owes me. I helped him bury a story about his son's run-in with a Brazilian model, her drug lord ex-boyfriend, and plane filled with statues of the Virgin Mary that weren't exactly holy relics." Aideen added as she finished the text.

The three of us turn around at the sound of laughter coming from the other side of the apartment. Sophia and Jenny were doubled over laughing at the absurdity of Aideen's statement.

"Okay, my little darlings. I'm off. I believe that I have stocked the kitchen with enough carbs, candy, and booze for you all. Enjoy!"

"Bye!"

"I love your mom," Jenny said with a mouth full of M&Ms and a glass of Champagne in her hand.

"Don't we all," Sophia and I said at the same time.

"Jinx!" I shouted and ran out of reach before I got slapped in the arm as per Sophia's usual response to the term. I was not going to an interview with Theo Lord with a bruise on my arm.

True to her word, Aideen's text produced an interview at LORD Publications. All I had to do was submit my resume and a few writing samples. I was not exactly sure why they needed to see my writing, but I guessed it couldn't be the worst thing in the world to have them review it. When I went to meet Mr. Lord's head of Human Resources, I had a standard interview with no palm reading and in actual chairs. By the end of it all, the woman sitting across from me took off her glasses and rested them on the top of her head while she stared at me. Then she said, "You have the job. I have sat here with thirty-some-odd girls and I don't think that one of them knew how to answer a phone correctly. You. You have something. I can feel it. Be here at seven on Monday. I will get you all set up."

Both shocked and extremely giddy, I managed to get out, "Thank you so much. You will not be—"

But before I could finish she cut me off. "I know. I know. Just be here on time on Monday. Now get out of my office. I have some paperwork to do."

Grabbing all my stuff, I quickly headed out of the office and into the elevator. Feeling the smile grow to a freakish Joker level, I tried to calm myself down. A real job. I finally had a real job and I had Aideen to thank for this. Part of me hated that I used her influence to get me in the door. I have worked hard and did everything I was supposed to. Yet, I knew it was her connections that got me this job. Should I still take it? *Yes. It is not how you get the job but what you do when you have it.* For the first and last time in my life, I took advantage of some of the perks of knowing the right people.

It was five months before I met Patrick Lord in person. Sure, I knew who he was. I had heard all the gossip. Plus, Sophia and Margo loved to tell me about his escapades at the clubs when they were out looking for Mr. Right Now. He was the bad boy billionaire jetting around town on his Harley-Davidson Low Rider making the women swoon. However, when I finally met him for the first time, he was different than I expected.

It was a Friday just before five when he walked into the executive wing of LORD Publications with his sunglasses on, looking like he rolled out of someone's bed a mere hour before. I had known that he was going to see his father that day because I set up the meeting for noon with his assistant. I even confirmed with her this morning to make sure that he would be showing up so I could have lunch delivered right before he came in. She assured me that he would be there. Not so much.

"Hello, darling," he said while sitting on the edge of my desk. "Patrick Lord to see—"

"I know who you are and you are late. Your father is on a conference call with Claudia and Japan."

"Ah. Japan, huh? The whole country on the phone with the golden child and Dear Old Dad. What a call that must be." As he moved his sunglasses to his head, I could see the dark circles under his eyes. It looked like he hadn't slept in a month.

"They…uh…Japan…the marketing division over there is trying…" I was a babbling idiot. "Why don't I get you some coffee. It looks like you need it."

"Thanks, love."

"PATRICK!" a loud booming voice came from the inside of Mr. Lord's office.

"You rang," Patrick mocked as he walked through the door.

"Don't be smart with me, young man. Hold on. Camilla, come in here."

I should have been used to this. For five months, the man barked orders through his glass walls. I had started to figure out that it is just how he liked to operate. It was nothing personal, just him. Standing up, I smoothed out my skirt and checked my new blonde bob for any flyaways. I had just gotten the haircut right before I started. It made me look like a completely different person and I liked that.

"Mr. Lord," I said, trying desperately not to make eye contact with the six-foot-two British god that was now lounging on the couch in his father's office. Even haggard and hung over, he still looked damn good.

"Have you filed the work with Legal that I left on your desk?" Theo asks without looking up from the papers on his desk.

"Yes, sir."

"What about the marketing? Have you sent the response to the promotional images that they submitted earlier today?"

"That was done about an hour ago and I made sure that they knew you wanted more options for a younger demographic. Also, your schedule is updated for next week. The appointment with your ex-wife's lawyer was rescheduled for two weeks from Tuesday, and your plane tickets for the trip to London are purchased and in your bag."

"Where can I get me one of you?" Claudia chimed in with a smirk. She hadn't had an assistant that lasted more than two weeks in over five years. Human Resources was running out of hiring options because the word was out that Claudia was difficult. I believe the term Dragon Lady is what her assistants called her as they run into the elevator crying.

Completely dismissing his daughter's comment, he said, "Well then. I guess you can leave. Oh, and close the door on your way out. I want to speak with my children without interruption."

"Got it. Have a good weekend," I said as I left behind a room with so much tension they'd need a sledge hammer to get through it.

On Monday of the following week, I was getting set up

at my desk. Theo's schedule was always packed. Everyone wanted a piece of the boss, so I rarely had time to breathe. It helped that I was in the habit of arriving an hour before Mr. Lord, or anyone else for that matter, showed up. I needed that time so that I could get organized, have my checklist ready for the day, and actually eat something. Today, the muffin sitting next to my travel mug was calling my name.

I was startled when I heard a ding from the elevator, but it was who got off that made me nearly fall off my chair. It was Patrick. What the hell was he doing in the office at seven in the morning? No…what was he doing in the office period? I wondered if he even knew where his office was. Then our eyes met, and all thoughts left my brain for a minute.

"Somehow I had a feeling that you would be here."

"What gave me away?" I tried not to look back up in his eyes. Blue eyes do me in every time. Well, that and an accent. So basically, I was screwed here.

"For one. You are one of *those* girls," he said this with a heavy emphasis on *those*.

"Excuse me?" My head snapped up from my keyboard. "What the hell is that supposed to mean?"

"Calm down, love. It was a compliment. I meant that you are a career girl. I can see it in your eyes. You don't want to be Dad's assistant for the rest of your life and you aren't flirting with him, so there is no way you have your sights set on being wife numero three." He said as he waved three fingers back and forth in the air.

I did my best to not show my gag reflex when he mentioned dating his father, but I don't think I did such a good job because he burst out laughing.

"Pops not your type?"

"No. He most certainly is not. Not to mention I have a rule. I don't date people I work with."

"Well then! It is good that I don't *actually* do any work here. Now, do you have an idea where my office is?"

"Follow me." I got up from my desk, grabbing my coffee cup and shoving a piece of my muffin in my mouth. I was determined to show him my indifference to his charms, even if it wasn't true. "Right this way, Mr. Lord."

He shuddered. "Say it again."

"Say what?"

"Mr. Lord."

"Oh God." I couldn't help but roll my eyes. I stopped in front of his office, opened the door, and made a gesture with my hand to suggest he enter.

"You will be saying that soon enough," he whispered in my ear as he walked into the space that looked like it hadn't been used for a year.

"I don't know what type of women you are used to encountering, but… Oh wait, I do. In fact, everyone who has read a gossip magazine in the checkout line knows the type of women you date."

"You wound me." He placed his hand over his heart, feigning pain.

"I have a feeling you will heal just fine. And since I

am nowhere near a size-two model looking to land me a billionaire, using that tired line on me just isn't going to cut it. You are going to have to work a little harder than that. Have a nice day, Mr. Lord." I turned around and shut his door behind me. As soon as I got back to my workspace, I saw through the glass walls that he was sitting on the edge desk shaking his head. I was not going to make this easy for him. I had no intention of dating this man, but, there was no harm in a little fun...right?

Soon after that, Patrick's visits became more frequent. He started showing up for work and even beat me into the office a few times. I don't know if it was his meeting with his father or if he was starting to get bored with his laissez faire lifestyle, but he was digging in and putting in long hours at LORD. When I passed his office a few times, I never once saw anything but emails or layouts up on his screen. Shocking really. I always wondered what the one-eighty was really about, but he never answered when I asked, so I chose to let it go.

Our brief sessions of witty banter soon turned into me accepting his offer for lunch. Then there were a few dinners out at local hot spots. There were even a few moments in this office late at night that I am not incredibly proud of, but we were both unattached and I was determined to prove that blondes did indeed have more fun.

One night, he was walking me home and making fun of the way I ate my dinner. I tried to let it roll off my shoulders, but after the fourth snide comment, it was beginning to irk me. I have always been a little sensitive when people point out my relationship to food. As a once chubby girl, I used to battle with myself and my parents about what I was putting into my body. Finally, in college, I had gotten to a place where I could be healthy and happy with the way I looked. So, these particular jokes hit home though I knew there was no way he could know all of that.

Patrick continued his chiding of my eating habits as he said, "You know that it is not normal that you don't have your food touch and then stack up everything on your fork. They are touching!"

"I let my food touch." I took a brief pause. "It is just that sometimes I like to organize the plate before I eat it so that I can create the perfect bite."

"That is bloody crazy. You know that, right?"

"Yeah, but who are you to judge, Patty?" It was the first time I called him this. No one ever called him by the nickname. I found out one night when we were laying in his bedroom that his grandfather used to call him Patty. I loved it and started calling him that when we were alone. At first he bitched and moaned, but then he started to let it slide. To this day, I don't know if anyone else has called him that. "You take fifteen years to order a coffee and then you have them remove the whipped cream after you tell them to put it on."

"I guess we are all a little mad here." His cheshire grin got larger. "Oh look here! We walked all the way to my place. What a coincidence!"

"I don't believe in coincidences." I stated quite matter of factly. I was still a little pissed about the food comments.

"Then let's call it all part of my master plan."

Shaking my head, I followed him into the West End Avenue building, smiling at the doorman as he opened the door for us.

❧

Snap. Snap. Snap.

"Cam. Cami. Camilla Valentini."

"Sorry. What?" I look around and see Sophia snapping her finger in my face. Jenny, Margo, and Paula must have arrived while I was zoning out.

"Where did you go right now?" Jenny asks as she picks up the menu and starts to read.

"I know where she went. Right to the mattress," Sophia jokes as her eyebrows wiggle.

"She is fighting with someone?" Jenny asks.

"No. Not 'going to the mattresses.' She went back to her sexy time with Patrick Lord," Sophia adds.

"Oh… When was the last time you saw him?" Margo places her napkin on her lap as she waves over the waiter. "We are going to need a bottle of Moet. You know what? Make that two."

"We just ran into him," I say looking around as if

someone is listening to us. "I don't think he even knew who I was. It was six years ago."

"I call bullshit on that one." Sophia says as she taps her fingers on the table.

"I'm with Soph on this one. He remembers you," Margo says. "Damn. Has it been six years? We're getting old! Where's that waiter with my Champs?"

"What a manwhore," Jenny mumbles and we all start laughing.

"Seriously guys. I am not sure how memorable I am. Plus, I don't exactly look the same as I did back then. It was when I was blonde."

"Oh God. You dated him when you had that horrible bob thing with your hair? I can still smell the bleach thinking about it," Margo says.

"I don't think I would have recognized myself if I was in his position. We only dated for a month or so before I left LORD. And how many women has he dated since?"

"A lot," Sophia says.

"Not helpful, Soph. You know that was the closest thing to a relationship that Cami has had since—" Paula says before I can cut her off.

"Stop. Patrick was just fun. Can we talk about something else? Anything else?" I desperately try to think of a new topic of conversation.

"Oh, I forgot. Camilla Valentini, the permanent bachelorette until she hits her ten-year goal. You're a commitment phobe, babe. Accept it. Embrace it. Move on," Sophia blurts out.

"I'm not a commitment phobe."

"You do run any time a guy tries to make it more than casual," Paula says in the most matter-of-fact voice.

"I don't run," I say with a forced pout on my face. Just then a waiter came with five glasses filled to the top with Champagne. I was never happier to see anyone in my life.

"Okay. I think that we should leave Cami alone for a little bit. I mean, seeing that level of sexy up close and out in the wild would throw anyone off her game. So, let's toast to something." Margo holds up her glass.

"To going against the grain," Jenny starts.

"To loving tension, no pension," Sophia sings.

"To starving for attention," Margo says with a huge smile.

"To any passing fad," Paula reluctantly adds.

"To being an us for once... instead of a them!" I finish up.

"La vie bohème." We all clink our glasses and smile. *Rent* was the first Broadway play that we all went to see together and each of us have the DVD sitting on our book shelves. It is our go-to toast when we need to lighten up the mood or are too drunk to say anything else.

Three hours later, we have worked our way through the most amazing selection of food I have ever tasted. From the amuse-bouche to creamy clam chowder to the perfectly cooked pork with a balsamic plum reduction to the sinfully chocolate dessert—I am in heaven.

Margo couldn't be beaming more if she made the food. It's difficult for her to evaluate a client's work objectively when she is promoting it 24-7. But as we all devour plate after plate of the chef's specialties, it's clear to all of us that this place has all the makings of New York's next *It* place.

"Now remember to hit up all your social media and tell them about this meal. Paula, you have over twenty thousand followers that I want salivating over this food."

"No problem," Sophia says while taking out her phone and posting an image to Instagram of the empty plate sitting on the table in front of her.

"Done." Jenny types into her phone as the sound of a bird goes off into the distance, delivering her tweet to her followers.

"I will write something up after I get back to my desk," Paula adds.

"Cami. How about you?" Margo asks.

"Uh…" I try to come up with something, but I have nothing.

"Margo. You know Cami is a social media virgin. She doesn't have any accounts except for a Facebook that has about twenty people on it. Most of those are family," Jenny says.

"Wait. You don't have any social accounts besides that sad, sad Facebook profile?" Margo asks.

"I have LinkedIn too," I add as the lamest defense ever.

"Don't even." Margo holds up her hand as she chugs the remainder of her drink. "We are going to have a long talk, young lady, and you will be setting up accounts. I mean, you are in your twenties, not your sixties. Where is your social relevance?"

"My seventy-five-year-old grandmother has 'the Twitter' and an Instagram account." Jenny says partially in jest, but I know her grandmother is extremely into her online persona.

"You are not helping, Jen." I give her a good kick in the leg, but then Paula screams out in pain. "Sorry! I was trying to get that one."

"And that, ladies and gentlemen, is why I sit cross-legged or with my leg under my butt and the other to the side." Jenny grins.

"Oh. So I am not the only one that finds you annoying. There are others that try to kick you under the table as well?"

Jenny glowers at me before she picks up the wrapper from her gum and throws it at my head.

"And that is our cue to leave." Paula raises her hand to get the waiter to come over.

"Don't you dare. This one is on me. It is a business expense." Margo winks.

Standing outside in the cold, I hear a bing from inside my purse. It is most likely a text from my mom, so it can wait until we all say our goodbyes. As soon as Sophia and I turn the corner, I pull out my phone. She is already tapping away, responding to all her Instagram comments about the restaurant, so I figure I will just let my mom know I am alive. Then I see it. It is the reminder I had set about the Human Resources meeting tomorrow. With everything that happened, I completely forgot about it.

"What's the face for?" Sophia looks up from her phone.

"Nothing. It is my alarm. I must have put in the time wrong when I was setting it all up yesterday. You know my head hasn't been focused. I will fix it later," I say hoping that my lame excuse will pass the Sophia test.

"Yeah…no. I am not buying that one, but since it is so cold that my tits are going to fall off, I will let this one slide until we are indoors."

Later that night I sit in my room and start thinking about the meeting tomorrow. Suddenly, I have an uneasy feeling. I should have gone to Ethel in HR as soon as the incident happened. Why had I not documented all the crap that Joel has put me through these past years? This was going to bite me in the ass…I just knew it.

Chapter Ten

I CAN HEAR THE ALARM ON MY PHONE GO OFF AS I lie on my bed. It had been a long night of tossing, turning, pacing and running through every possible outcome of today's meeting. If I managed to get an hour's worth of sleep, it was a lot. I wish I had a crystal ball to know how all of this is going to turn out. The fact that I am not sure how it will turn out is giving me panic attacks.

With the alarm still playing *Cannon in D Major*, I know that I need to get up. As soon as my feet hit the floor, it is as if I am a robot. I take a shower, go to Sophia's closet to pick out the most business outfit she has that will fit me, and proceed with military precision to put on my makeup and do my hair. By the time I'm ready, Sophia is in the kitchen pouring herself and me coffee.

"Ahh… Thank God for coffee," I manage to say as I take a sip. The first taste of coffee in the morning is always the best.

"You are welcome. How did you sleep last night?" she asks, looking up from her newspaper.

"You heard me pacing, didn't you?"

"Yeah. I was working most of the night and when I passed by your room I could hear you muttering. I figured you were running things through in your head like you used to before a big test back in college."

"I just don't know what to do. I keep going through all the outcomes of today, but I have no idea what Ethel is going to say. And on top of that, I keep beating myself up for not saying something about the perv's behavior sooner. I figured it would eventually stop or he would move on to the next girl."

"Obviously, you underestimated his ability to be skeevy to more than one woman at once."

"Guess so." I reach over and grab a croissant from the plate lying on the counter. "What if they…"

"Stop it right now. You are being a whiny ass and I will not have it. What happened to the Cami that stormed the dean's office with her petition filled with signatures to save a professor's job?"

"I didn't storm the dean's office. I set a meeting and talked with her with my bullet points in hand."

"Fine. Ruin my idealized version of you, but still, you were composed and even though you were nervous, you still were able to get things done."

"But that was for someone else. Not me."

"Are you saying that you have cojones the size of bowling balls when you are dealing with other people's battles, but you can't manage to grow a pair to fight your own battles?"

"Soph…"

"Don't you dare Soph me. I am going to be your friend right now and tell you that all the crap that is flying around in your head needs to be shelved. Make a list of things that you know is true and walk in there with the facts. You are good at that. Organize your thoughts and think before you say anything. Don't let your worry or anger get the better of you."

"I know. You are right."

Sophia looks at me knowing that I am just trying to make her stop talking and let me leave. Yet she continues. "I know that you are still off balance from the fire less than three days ago and you are freaking out with all the what-ifs. But now is the time to put on your big girl panties and put yourself first. You need to stand up for yourself. You can't expect anyone else to do that but you. That pervert violated your space. You are the victim in this situation. He does not have power over you unless you give it to him. And for that matter…"

"Okay. Okay. I got it. Short version. I need to grow a pair and breathe." Giving Sophia a big hug, I take a huge bite of the rest of my croissant and walk out the door. *Stop being so nervous. I can do this.*

$$\text{———}\mathcal{Q}\text{———}$$

At 9:15AM, I am sitting in a chair opposite Ethel Rosenberg, the head of Human Resources. This woman has been in the position since the dawning of time from what I can tell. She is eighty years old, but not in a granny type of way. Her hair is that amazingly stunning silver that few women get as they age, styled perfectly with soft curls that frame her face and her outfit is vintage Channel with just the right amount of jewelry to accessorize the look. Suddenly, my outfit isn't looking as posh as I thought it did when I walked out of the townhouse this morning. I need to get clothes soon. Everything from Sophia's closet is at least one size too small for me. The pencil skirt I am wearing is held closed with two linked safety pins, and when I sit, this blue button-down blouse is busting open exposing the lace of my bra. Not exactly business professional attire.

"Ms. Valentini. I am glad you could make it today. I know last week you decided to work from home."

"Yes. Sal gave me permission. In truth, I get so much more work done when I am not in the office."

"Well, be that as it may, we do not pay you to sit home

in sweatpants and occasionally submit your work." Ethel opens a file that is on her desk and sighs.

"I think that you are making the wrong conclusion about my work ethic, Mrs. Rosenberg. I—"

"It is Ms. Rosenberg."

Of course it is.

"And I am just stating that when you were hired to work here, it was to work in this office at a desk provided to you by this company. It was not for you or anyone else to complete the work assigned from a remote location."

"Or anyone else? I am sorry, ma'am, but are you saying that I was not the one doing the work that I turned in last week."

"Well, you see. We have had a complaint made against you. A staff member felt verbally abused and bullied by you. This person also insinuated that you might be farming out your work to others so that you could have more time to…how was it put…ah yes. So, that you would have more time to be more social with people who can get you out of the copy editor's chair."

"Say what now?"

"We do not take bullying or aggressive behavior lightly, Miss Valentini. It is a serious accusation. Not to mention this unfortunate business with you not doing your work yourself. I am afraid that…"

I cannot believe this is happening. "Ms. Rosenberg. Before you go any further, I feel that I have the right to know who my accuser is."

"I don't think that is necessary in this case. He is a senior staffer that we all respect very much."

I choke a little before I get out. "If it is Joel who said this, I think that you should know that he has been sexually harassing me since my first day at this job. Then last week, he took it too far, so I responded in the only way I could. I told him he didn't have a chance with me and that he was a pervert."

Ethel lets out a heavy sigh as a small piece of her hard-as-nails attitude begins to fade. "Camilla. Do you mind if I call you that?"

"Sure."

"Joel said that you would make up a story like this. He feels that the only way for you to truly learn that your behavior has consequences is for you to be terminated from your job here at *Exhibition*."

"Seriously?" My hands are gripping the arms of the chairs so tightly that I think I might leave finger indentations in them.

"I am sorry, Camilla. As of today, you are no longer working at *Exhibition*. I will have Tony take you to your desk to collect your personal items and then I ask that you leave the premises with as little incident as possible."

"You are firing me? You are firing me!" My voice gets increasingly louder as a large man with no neck that I can see appears in the doorway.

"Please don't make a scene Ms. Valentini."

"That sleazy excuse for a human being puts his hands

on me and tries to blackmail me into going out with him and I am losing my job?"

"If what you are saying is true, why didn't you come to me after it happened?"

"I needed time to process everything. I was planning to contact you, but then I got your email. Over the years, I thought I could handle it on my own. I worked hard and never did anything that would jeopardize my career here. I just…"

Ethel gets up from her desk and does something that completely shocks me. She puts her arm around me and hugs me. Then as she is pulling away she says in the most hushed tones, "You are not the only one. Trust me. It is better for you that you leave now. This situation could get far worse if you continue to fight it. I will do what I can about your permanent work record. Take care, Camilla."

"Thank you." I move away from her with utter disbelief. This woman who I thought was cold as ice is showing compassion. It even appears she knew what was going on all along. *Why wouldn't she do anything about it? For that matter, why didn't I?* I turn to Tony as he gives me a half-hearted smile and walks me to what used to be my desk.

Taking a few extra minutes to make sure that I have everything that is mine, I look at the desk I've spent four years at.

"Cami?" Janice's voice questions.

"Hon. You okay? We all just heard in the meeting that you were leaving."

"Yeah. I am fine."

"For what it's worth, we all know that this was not your fault. It is just that when you are the son of the editor-in-chief you have a lot more pull. And we—"

"You don't have to say it. You have a family to support and I wouldn't want anyone else to be collateral damage from this. I stood up to him and now I am fired."

"Karma is a bitch, sweetie. Remember that." Janice gives me a pat on the arm and walks back to her desk.

A few other people that I've worked with over the years come over and say their goodbyes. The rest of them can barely look at me. I don't know if they believe the BS that Joel is spewing or if they just can't face me knowing that they did nothing to stop it. Really, it doesn't matter. This is what it is. For the first time in my life, I am left with the overwhelming feeling that I have nothing to ground me. My home is a pile of rubble and the one thing that has been driving me my entire life has just been taken away from me.

Then I see him. He is standing at his doorway with his arms crossed and a smile on his face. It takes all my strength not to drop the box of my belongings and punch him in that smarmy mug of his. But I am not going to let him win. I stand up straight, smile at him, and walk onto the elevator. Then as soon as the doors shut, I slide down the wall behind me and start to cry.

Chapter Eleven

"CAMI, YOU HOME?" SOPHIA'S VOICE IS ECHOING down the hallway.

I have successfully managed to avoid her and everyone else all day by burrowing under the comforter with the curtains drawn and my phone off. I am not in the mood to talk to anyone or explain what happened. If I did, she will call everyone over and they will try to make it better. But for right now, I don't want it to be better. I just want to wallow in the fact that I have no home, no job, and at this moment, no plan. I have been played by a manipulative self-indulgent slime ball and should have known better. All I want to do is lie here and eventually fall asleep. Then when I wake up tomorrow, I will deal with everything.

"Cami?" A bit of light shines across my bed as she cracks the door open.

"I am not in here. Try down the hall."

"Very funny. I am guessing today didn't go that well. Why didn't you come and get me in my studio?"

"Soph. I just can't right now. I want to sleep."

"Sure. I...uh...I am going to go meet the girls for drinks."

"Please don't tell them anything." I jump to sit upright.

"How can I tell them anything? You haven't told me shit." Her tone is getting angrier than I would have expected, but we have been through a lot over the years and she deserves the truth.

"Fine. Here is the short of it. I lost my home in a fire and explosion. You already know that. Now, as the olive in the martini, I don't have a job any longer." Sophia just stares at me. "Oh, and my professional reputation might be in the crapper because Joel told HR that I bullied him at work and farmed out my work to others. Apparently, I am a big ass kisser and will do anything to spend time with the rich and famous to advance my career."

"That sniveling son of a bitch! I am going to kill him." She gets up from the bed where she was while I was giving her the synopsis of my life and heads down the hallway.

"Soph? What are you doing?" I quickly follow her and I notice that she is in the kitchen eyeing the knives. "Sophia Maeve Pollock! Get out of the kitchen right now."

"You need to let me do something about this, Cami."

"I don't need anyone to do anything. I will figure it out. I hope…"

"You can't let him get away with this. We should call Paula. She will know what to do." Sophia reaches for her phone.

"Stop," I say in the most forceful tone I can muster up. I am running on an hour sleep and am completely drained. "I do not need this right now. I am dealing with my own crap and trying to figure out what just happened. I can't have everyone else involved in this. I just…" I start crying again. Twenty-six years of life and I can count on two hands how many times I cried, but now I am unable to control the waterworks.

"It's okay. Sorry. You know me. I am more of an act now kind of girl. I never think about the consequences until I am in a tight spot or prison. Don't you remember when my ex cheated on me with that bimbo from one of those reality shows on MTV?"

"Oh. I had forgotten about that one. You were never formally charged for that right?"

"Nope. The officer who was called to the scene hated

the show and let me off with a warning. Hindsight, I should have never let him get under my skin. Just like now. He who shall never be named again isn't worth it."

"I know. But honestly, I just need to be a blob of emotions right now. I can't think or deal with anyone else's opinion."

"You're right. They might just go completely off the handle and you don't need that." With a side glance and a smile, Sophia stands up in front of me and picks her phone back up. "So how about Chinese food, booze, and a *Buffy* marathon?"

"That sounds better than you will ever know."

"Let me just text the girls and tell them I am bailing on tonight. They shouldn't make a big deal out of it because I was supposed to be working anyway."

"I am going to put on leggings and a sweater from your closet. If we are having Chinese, I need pants with some give." Looking down, I realize that I had curled into bed with the outfit I wore to *Exhibition*.

"Valid point. I should take a quick shower before we start too. I reek of turpentine."

"Soph," I say as she turns around. "Thank you."

"You don't have to thank me. Just have the wine open and a glass filled on my return."

Chapter Twelve

I MADE IT FOR AS LONG AS I COULD, BUT I REALLY didn't get much sleep last night and staring at the patterns on the wallpaper is starting to make me go crazier than I already am. One would think two bottles of wine and enough greasy food to feed a small nation would have sent me right to sleep, but I managed to watch the first five episodes of *Buffy* from season one while Sophia was snoring in the love seat next to me. It wasn't until about three that I cleaned up the empty bottles and containers and headed back to my bedroom.

As I reach for my phone on the night table, I see that it is five. Now is as good a time as any to get up. Last night was a good distraction from my life. Nothing makes you feel better about what is going on around you then watching *Buffy*. The poor girl had to fight supernatural forces, stop the Hellmouth from opening, and manage not to flunk out of high school. Plus, the guy she is into is a vampire with a curse on him. Makes my drama look far less interesting. Leave it to Buffy and her Sunnydale gang to put it all into perspective.

Today, I am going to get things figured out. Sure, I had a setback, but I can do this. I will start with a walk around Central Park to clear my head and go through my phone messages. There were about nineteen unanswered emails and texts that I should respond to at some point. Then a much needed trip to Bloomingdales. A little retail therapy courtesy of my last paycheck at *Exhibition* will make things a bit more manageable.

When I get back, I will start compiling a list of potential jobs and companies that will fit into my ten-year plan. I am not starting from square one this time. I have four years of experience, so it might be better this time around. Maybe I can even sign on to a couple of those sites that send you emails about potential openings in your field. My resume needs to be updated, but that shouldn't be too bad. I have a few freelance gigs that will need to be added, but I have worked for the same company for years. It was supposed to lead the way to bigger and better things. Instead it left me with wondering if it was all worth it. I hope that Ethel will be able to remove all the crap that Joel reported to her. It seemed like she might. Just in case though, I will come up with something to tell future employers.

As I step out into the fresh cold air, I take a deep breath. I can do this. I know I can. This is just a slight derailment from the plan, but I can do this. *How many times can you say it to make it true, Cami?* If I say that enough, maybe I might believe it.

"Hey watch it, love." A man bumped into my arm.

"You are the one who bumped into me and…Patrick." As I look into my reflection in his sunglasses, I can see just how exhausted I look.

"Camilla. Everything alright?" Patrick lifts his glasses to the top of his head and looks at me with concern.

"I'm…I…I don't know."

"I know that I am not the go-to guy for emotions and such, but if you need—"

"Don't. Patrick. I just can't have you being nice to me right now. We haven't seen each other in years and now you want to…what…act like we are friends? You don't have to pretend that you care." As soon the words come out of my mouth, I realize what a brat I am being. I should have stayed in bed.

"Easy there." He raises his hands in surrender. "I was just offering an ear. You look like you could use someone to talk to, or a stiff one. Personally, I would go for the drink."

I pull out my cell phone to look at the time. "Shouldn't you be going to work?"

"Just on my way now." He points to the motorcycle sitting at the curb.

"Didn't you live on the West Side?" For the life of me, I don't know why I am continuing this conversation. I should be walking away, but there is some comfort in standing here with him.

"Not any more. I bought this place a few months ago. The co-op board was a bitch to get past, but when you have the great Theo Maclaren Lord as your father, they tend to loosen up a bit. What about you? I thought you lived down on the Lower East Side."

"I did. My apartment blew up. I am staying with Sophia." I take in a deep breath as my eyes start to tear. *Here I go again.*

"Holy crap. That was your place? I saw that in the news."

"Yeah, and to add insult to injury, I am now currently unemployed." I manage to say as I start to cry and laugh at the same time. I just can't hold it in any more. Every emotion that I have is coming out.

"Camilla? Are you okay?" Patrick looks as if he doesn't know whether to console me or run the other way.

"No. I am not okay. Everyone wants me to be, but…" I can't hold it in any more. I start laughing.

"Is this an American thing? What am I missing?"

"No. It is…" I chuckle and throw my arms up. "I am screwed. I have nothing. No home of my own. No job. And to put the cherry on top, my Aunt texted me that I have to wait six months before I can touch my trust fund. Apparently, it is under review by the Federal Government or something."

"Seriously? Bloody hell."

"Yeah. I don't know what I am going to do." I say as I start to stare down the street. Today things look so different than they used to. I see the garbage lined on the curbs as the blaring sounds of horns pierce my ears. *What happened to my New York?*

"I know what you need." He waggles his eyebrows.

"Patrick. I am not going to sleep with you."

"Though that would be wonderful and I hope that we can table that for another time, I was going to suggest we get some pancakes. I know the best place."

"Don't you have to work?"

"The beauty of being the boss. Now get on the bike."

"Uh. Let me think about that. Nope."

"Come on."

"It's cold. I'm mentally spent. I can't Patrick. I just need to go for a walk."

"Cami, I am not leaving you alone this morning, so if you will not get on the bike, let's head down the street and see where we can grab something."

"Oh really? So, I don't have a say in this at all?" I

try to put up a fight, but I just can't handle witty banter today. "I know that you don't remember much about our time together, but ultimatums don't exactly work so well with me."

"I remember more than you think." He smirks. Then as his eyes look into mine, I can see all the bluster in him begins to fade to sincerity. I don't know how, but he used to be able to read me better than my family and friends ever could.

Realizing that he is not going to give up, I concede and we head down the street.

☙

"What can I get ya, hon?" the waitress asks with her pad at the ready.

"We will have two coffees and your morning special with extra blueberry jam on the side," Patrick orders.

"You got it."

"I could have ordered for myself, you know."

"I am well aware of your ability to take care of yourself, but you would have ordered something like a fruit salad with toast and that is not going to cut it if you are going to tell me what is going on with you."

"What do you mean? I'll be fine."

"Bollocks. You just lost your home and your job. I may not remember a lot, but I remember you. This has to be sending you into a world of chaos in your head. Now tell Dr. Patrick the whole story and we will see what we can do about it."

At that moment, I remember why I fell for Patrick Lord. I guard my heart very carefully when it comes to the opposite sex. After Joseph, I never wanted to feel that level of hurt again, so I decided to keep men at arm's length. Patrick was the only guy to come close to breaking down my walls, but I don't know how I would cope if I let Patrick in now. What we had back then meant something to me, but I never knew if it could have become something more. And now…there is just too much going on. *I can't. Can I?*

For all the bravado and bad boy bullshit he shows the rest of the world, he is so much more than that. He was so much more than that to me. Besides being off-the-charts smart, he has a huge heart for the people that he cares about. There is not anything that he will not do for his family. I have seen him stand up for Claudia and little brother, Theo Jr., with his father. Being a Lord meant being in the spotlight which is not the easiest thing. Sometimes, I used to think that he tried to get into trouble with the press to try and give his siblings a break from being hounded. The only time when he wasn't in the spotlight was when his grandfather was sick. Patrick was the one that stayed home with him to make sure that he was getting the care he needed. People said that he was shipped off to rehab, but in reality, he was in Nantucket with a handful of doctors and nurses seeing to the final months of his grandfather's life.

As I sit at the table recanting the latest events of my life, he is listening. He doesn't check his phone or check out the hot girls walking by the windows gawking at him. He is giving me his full attention and it scares the shit out of me.

"So that is about all of it."

"All of it. I would say. If I had the connections, I would put a hit out on that little arsehole."

"Stop it. Are you going to eat that?" I reach over and grab a slice of bacon from his plate.

"Apparently not."

"Sorry. I am starving. And everything is better with bacon."

"That it is. That it is." The anger on his face from the whole Joel situation recap is plain to see. I know that he has never liked the guy, because of the way he treats women. Patrick may be a playboy, but he never disrespects women. "He is such an arse. It is part of the reason why I would never do business with him or his father. And we have all heard the rumors about his father having to pay off women, but he needs to be…"

"Neutered," I state bluntly.

"Well, there is that." He shoves an impressive amount of pancakes into his mouth.

Sitting across from Patrick is as if six years haven't passed. I almost forget he is the guy who stopped returning my phone calls and left me with so many questions all those years ago.

"So. Shouldn't you be getting back to LORD?"

"Indeed. What are you going to do today on your first day of freedom?"

"I wouldn't exactly put it like that. I was going to go for a walk this morning to clear my head and then do some shopping because Sophia's closet is only going to take me so far. However, *someone* derailed that plan."

"You will survive."

"I guess I will just walk through the park and then make my way down Madison Avenue."

"Sounds like as good a day as any. Claudia has worn out the metal strip on her credit card on her walks down the avenue to reprioritize her life." He waves the waitress over to get the check and shoves a pile of bills in under the receipt.

"I bet. To think of your sister's closet, I bet I could have a shoegasm just by walking into it."

"Now that is something I would like to see." We both stand up and head out the door.

"Very funny." I lightly smack his arm as if it were the most natural thing in the world. There is an ease between us and at this moment, it is a bit unnerving. I don't need this right now. I have other things to figure out before I add someone else into my life. Yet…I can't help but feel a little flush when we touch. There is something about Patrick that gets to me.

"Listen, Cami. I say this from the bottom of my blackened heart." He pauses for my eye roll. "If you need anything, call me."

"But I don't have your number," I say waving my phone.

"But I have yours and I just sent you a message. Save the number under the best shag of your life just in case you can't remember who it is from."

"And there he is, ladies and gentlemen. The man that every tabloid loves to talk about. Wait. How did you get my number?"

He smiles as he walks back to his motorcycle, leaving me in front of the diner to contemplate…

"Sophia," I mumble. "She is a dead woman."

After spending the better portion of the day walking around New York and doing some much needed shopping, I have a little bit of my old self back. In the dressing room of Lavin, I took out my phone and started to compile a complete list of to-do's for when I got to Sophia's place. There was no way I'm going to let anyone stop me from getting where I want to be.

Sitting with my list, my laptop and a cup of coffee, I am relishing the quiet. There is a sticky note on the fridge telling me that Sophia is at a meeting with a potential patron and not to wait up, so the place is all mine. It is the first time since the fire that I have truly been alone and I need this. It isn't that I don't love my friends or the buzz of the city, but I like being alone. Margo says I am an introvert at heart, but I think it is that I am comfortable with myself. Much to my family's horror, I don't need anyone else to complete me. Sorry, Renée Zellweger.

The only things that I need right now are this cup of coffee and a job. I can't worry about an apartment until I figure out my finances and hear back from my Aunt. Sophia's is just going to have to be home base for a while. Maybe I can pay her rent in eggplant parmesan and tiramisu.

Now, first things first, I need to get back on track. Opening up my browser, I hold my cup in one hand as I type with the other. Fingers crossed…and maybe toes too, just in case.

Chapter Thirteen

I AM IN THE ROOM THAT I HAVE NOW CALLED HOME for about six months, staring at my computer screen, willing something to show up in my email box. Nothing. I press the envelope icon again. Nothing. Then I click on it continuously until I see that something is coming through. This could be it, but it is not. It is an email telling me that I am the beneficiary to a relative I may not even know I have in Kuala Lumpur. All I have to do is send them one hundred dollars to this off-shore account and...delete.

It has been the same thing day in and day out. There has not been one bite since I was fired from *Exhibition*. Over two hundred resumes have been mailed out to potential employers. I have sent follow-up emails to the applications. Nothing. Absolutely nothing was happening. I even went as far as to call my email provider to make sure that my emails were working. The very nice tech, Mary, on the other end of the phone reassured me that everything was working. Secretly, I wanted her to tell me that there was something wrong with my account. At least then I would be able to blame the lack of response on that instead of the simple fact that I was not what people wanted.

About a month or so into the search, I went through the stage when I thought that Joel was black balling me from the industry. I was convinced that he was talking to all his buddies and telling them about this prude he got canned from his Dad's magazine. Then I remembered that he was only important in his head and his reach into the real publishing world was not that long. He wouldn't have enough pull to get major publishing houses to shelve my resume.

The only time I got a response was when an editor from an online magazine called me because they were looking for someone to edit articles for their most popular column, *His City*. It is a dating column from the perspective of a gay man living in the city. It sounded interesting enough, so the managing editor and I agreed to a test run. They sent me an article and the level of *detail* into this man's sexcapades was astonishing. However, I needed the work, so I did what I needed to do. The two days after submitting my edits, I heard back from the magazine. They didn't like my comments and the way that I tweaked some of the sentence structures. It appears that I just don't have the mindset of a twenty-two year old gay man.

My life has become a routine. I get up, make coffee, throw my hair, most of the time dirty, on the top of my head, and sit in my room for hours on end, applying for any positions in publishing, many of which I am over qualified for. Then I lie in bed for hours wondering who I slighted in a former life to be going through this and wallow in my own patheticness. I am a sad excuse. I know it, but at this point, I have just embraced the suck.

I have stopped caring about what I look like and only do laundry when the bin is so filled with yoga pants, tanks, and t-shirts that I cannot fit any more. Lucky for me, Sophia has a washer and dryer in the basement, so I don't have to go out into public with the people who are actually contributing to society. I have become a shell of who I was. I don't go out anymore with my friends. They try to keep me in the loop, but after months of not responding to texts and phone calls, they know that I am just going to avoid them. Yet every day Sophia tries to make me get out of my head and see that I can be more. She leaves sticky notes with stupid drawings or quotes on my coffee cup. She comes into my room and opens the curtains to let the light in on the few moments that I am not shut up in there. She even has left flowers on my dresser to try to make me smile. I have to give her credit; she is not giving up on me. Though I guess I never gave up on her, so we have that in common. There have been attempts to lure me out with wine and *Gilmore Girls* reruns. Unfortunately for her, the promise of a Luke and Lorelai hookup cannot get me out of the funk that I am in.

Today, the weather app on my phone is telling me that it is ninety degrees and a typical humid August day. I am sitting at my computer, because really, where else would I be. I weed through the junk emails and check out the job sites for anything new. For some reason, I open a Word document and stare at the blank screen. The cursor is taunting me as it just blinks at me.

I wonder what all the planning was for. All the lists and the time spent figuring out where I would be in five or ten years. *You know where you will be in ten years, Cami? Sitting in this same exact place.* The shit hit the fan and I have not been able to see past what I lost. I try. I really do, but something is stopping me. Every day, I think that today will be different. Yet every day I wake up and am smacked in the face with everything I don't have. I don't have a job. I don't have a purpose. I don't have a man in my life. Sure, the last one is just something that I have recently added into the mix. Sophia has started to see a guy that has real staying power, as she likes to say. Seeing them together around the townhouse is difficult. I am happy for her, really, but I can't help think that it is just one more thing that I don't have.

I hate that I am becoming someone I don't even recognize anymore. I look at what others have and can't help but compare my life to theirs. I hate myself for the depressive state I am in and all the self-loathing that goes on in my head, but I just don't see a way out. For so many years, I planned everything and saw value in that. Now, I just can't. I see all the things that didn't happen for me.

This part of who I am has always haunted me. When I was younger, I was never enough. I would compare myself to others and measure myself by what they had. It is why I have always been so driven by my plans. I learned to cope with my feelings of insecurity and being less than what I imagined people wanted me to be by having control. I would organize my room to the point of being OCD. Nothing could be out of place or I couldn't sleep. I needed my own space where everything was exactly where I wanted it to be. It was the same with my apartment. I had comfort in the knowing that every-thing is exactly as it should be. I would make lists and go over them ten times to make sure I had everything that I needed to accomplish. Then I would systematically check off each item when they were done, only to start all over again the next day.

In recent years and many therapy sessions later, I have been able to ease up on my desire to prove that I am worthy by having control over my life. However, with everything that happened back in February, I have regressed right back to the girl who isn't enough. Emotions that I thought I worked through are coming back into my head. I wasn't the girl who was able to stop her fiancé from taking his own life. I wasn't enough for him. I will never be enough for anyone. I do not have the strength to hold myself together now.

The problem is that I don't seem to care. I suppose that seeing my indifference as a problem is a step in the right direction, but I have given into the lack of control. I have stopped trying to make everything perfect. Perfection is bullshit.

I sit and question all of my decisions. Why didn't I let my parents help me get an apartment on the Upper East side like they wanted? Should I have never left LORD Publications? Would I be on track with my plan if I didn't hook up with Patrick all those years ago? Should I have turned Joel in sooner? Every action and choice that I have made seems to be under interrogation.

Ugh! Snap out of this, Cami.

Trying to distract myself, I pick up my phone and run through my contacts. Then I type in P and wait for his name to show up. I am not going to call him, but seeing Patrick's name on my phone makes me wonder.

He has tried to reach out to me since I saw him last. I even got a text that said he had an idea for a job that I might find interesting, but could I really go back to working for LORD? Not that I left on bad terms or anything, but I don't want his father thinking that I am leveraging my relationship with Patrick to get a job with the company. It was bad enough that Theo found out about Patrick and I all those years ago. It was why I made the decision to quit. I didn't want to, but I knew that it was only a matter of time before people at LORD started talking. Plus, there was something about Claudia and Theo's reaction to the news that never sat well with me. They weren't upset, but there was something…was it doubt or maybe concern? I found the job at *Exhibition* on Craigslist which should have been my first red flag, but the site wasn't as sketchy as it is now. Although, in hindsight…

Putting down the phone, I look around the room filled with papers, piles of clothes, books littering almost every surface, and even some old coffee cups. *This is not me.* The girl who couldn't go to sleep without having everything in her bedroom put away wouldn't be able to function in this room. *This is not me.* I repeat this again and again as I sink down onto the floor. The tears stream down my face as I am overwhelmed with emotions that I cannot contain. *This is not me.*

Knock. Knock. Knock.

"Cami? You in here?" Sophia asks as she pokes her head through the crack in the door.

"Where else would I be? Hold on one sec. I have to just hit send on this email."

She walks into the room and sits on the edge of the bed, picking up a dirty t-shirt with her pointer finger and thumb while shaking her head. She looks for a place to put it, but cannot seem to see anywhere it could go. Standing up, I grab the shirt and throw it into the hamper already overflowing with clothes.

"You know I love you, right?"

"Yes…"

"God. I can't do this." She gets up, opens the curtains, and turns back to me. "You have to go take a shower. You are starting to smell. I can't think."

"Do I offend?" I put my nose down to my shoulder and take a whiff. "Woah. I think you are right. I didn't realize."

"Yeah. You haven't realized several things over the past months."

"Okay. I get it."

"No. The thing is that you don't get it. Now, go take a shower and then come out into the living room when you are dressed."

"Fine."

I have to admit taking the shower feels really good. It had been a few days and my hair was stuck to my head. As soon as I step into my room, it hits me. The mess. The clutter. The…what the hell is that on the floor? *Did it just move?* Not wanting to deal, I quickly throwing on the last pair of clean shorts and my HOW YOU DOIN tank top, I shut the door, and shuffle down the hallway. Then I hear it. The mumbles of more than one person and then "Shhhhhh. I think she is coming."

Entering the living room, it takes a minute for my eyes adjust to a volume of light. After blinking a few times, I see that all of my friends, my Aunt JoJo, and Patrick are sitting in the living room. Patrick… *Who called him? Sophia.*

"I don't believe this." I start to turn around to head back to my room.

"Cami. Just wait." Paula stands. "Please. Just sit. This will not take long. We are all just really concerned about you."

"This is ridiculous. I am not an alcoholic or a hoarder." I look around and Sophia clears her throat in protest. "I don't need. What is this? An intervention?"

"Dear. This is just a group of people who want to help you find your way back into the living." My Aunt JoJo comes over and gives me a hug. "Plus, we heard that there would be drinks after."

"Funny. Alright. Let's get this over with." I plop myself

down on the love seat and try not to make eye contact with Patrick. *Why is he here?*

"Cami. You know that we all love you and this isn't about making you feel bad, but you are not acting like yourself," Paula starts. "We all realize that you have been through a lot and we are not telling you how you should be coping with that. Yet…"

"Oh, cut the crap," Sophia interrupts. "The Cami I know would smack this version of you in the face. You sit in that room staring at a computer screen and feeling sorry for yourself. You are wallowing and it is pathetic. This is not you. The pile of crap in your bedroom is not you. What happened to the girl who had a plan?"

"I don't know," I say in a whisper barely audible.

"I know that you are searching for a job and it hasn't been going well."

"Hasn't been going well? Soph. It has been six months of endless emails and the only thing that I got contracted for was editing one article of gay softcore porn. And they didn't even want me anymore after I submitted it."

Patrick almost spits out his coffee as he burst out laughing. Soon we all join in at the bluntness of my statement.

"Love." Patrick turns to me. "I am probably the last person that you expected to see here, but Sophia thought I might be able to give an outsider's perspective. So, listen up. You are better than this. So what? Your plan went to shit. Shit. Happens. There isn't one of us that is sitting here that hasn't had an obstacle to overcome or have something that set them off down a path they wish they hadn't."

He's right. I hate that.

"Look at me. Do you really think that I want to be writing about entitled brats and celebrity antics? No offense," Bobby says while looking at Patrick. "I am not like the rest of you. I don't have a trust fund or my parents' money to fall back on. After college, I was presented with an option of taking a job so that I could eat and be able to pay rent or write what I wanted to. Now, I am obscenely overpaid for dishing crap that everyone loves to read, but very few actually care about. One choice has now lead me to doing something I never thought I would be able to. I am looking into starting my own magazine."

"What?" we all say in unison.

Bobby smiles. "My contract was up with *Exhibition* and after they treated you like that, I couldn't keep working for them. I told Sal and Joel to shove it. I have some money saved, so I am writing on my own blog for a while. It is just temporary until I figure out how to get my own publication up and running."

"Ooooh. Remember when Paula and I did the pop-up gallery in the middle of Union Square?" Jenny says. "It was so hot that a woman passed out and fell into our tent. She single handedly collapsed the whole thing. All of the paintings and sculptures damaged."

"I was in the tent at the time and got pinned by a giant cartoon character made out of old socks. We wound up having to buy all the art from the artists because most of it was damaged. It was a huge disaster," Paula adds. "There were a number of nights where a few bottles of wine magically disappeared in front of us. But that led to us realizing that if we wanted to have a gallery, we would have to go balls to the wall as Soph always says. We opened up Haut Monde Gallery that following year."

"I don't need to remind you of the horrible culottes debacle of 1995," Margo pipes up. "I will never be the same."

Sophia shakes her head as she sits right next to me. "And then there is me. Without you and most of the people in this room, I don't know where I would be right now. I went down a dark rabbit hole after my parents died. You were the one who was there every day making sure I was alive and you were the one that checked me into rehab." It was something that not many people knew about. In fact, it is the only secret that I have from my closest friends. Sophia was ashamed and I wanted to help her. So, we told the rest of the group that she was taking a vacation to clear her head with her family out in California. In reality, Sophia spent twenty-eight days detoxing and going to therapy only thirty minutes outside the city. I visited her three times for the group family sessions and to sneak her a scone from Alice's Tea Cup.

"You were where?" Jenny looks at Paula, Margo, and Bobby with a questioning glance.

"After the night with the party, Cami sat me down and gave me two options."

"Soph. You don't have to do this."

"Yes I do." Sophia looks at me and then out the window. "She said that I either got the help I needed or we couldn't be friends any longer. With everything going on after my parents died, I leaned on all of you a lot, but Cami has always been the one that I knew would always be there. Listening to her tell me that she would walk away from me and our friendship made me stop and think. I didn't want to admit that I had a problem or that I might not be coping the best. I just wanted to be numb. And in the back of my head, I knew that you all would be there for me if I fell." The shock on all their faces is startling, but expected. Sophia and I were always tight. They know that if I were to give her this ultimatum, I was at my breaking point.

"I remember the look on your face when I told you I couldn't take watching you fall apart. It was taking away bits of my heart every time I saw you like that." I grab her hand and squeeze.

"And now I am telling you that I can't watch you become someone that you are not meant to be. I want my hyper-organized control freak Cami back. Sure, she drove me bat shit crazy with all her to do lists and trips to the Container Store, but that is who you are. You have plans and all those damn lists you like to post up everywhere. When you get off course, you just re-evaluate and shift gears so that you can get to where you want to be. Look at me! I sound like one of those self-help gurus. But I digress." Sophia takes a swig of I don't know what and keeps going. "It is just like when you were seeing Patrick and you knew that you couldn't work for LORD any longer. You saw the way his father and Claudia looked at you and the whispers that were going on behind your back when everyone found out you two were dating. How many nights did we finish a bottle of wine each talking about what you should do? It was tearing you apart, but then you had enough. Sure, you wound up working for a douche nozzle that isn't fit to do anything but scratch his balls all day. I need you to put on your big girl panties and stop this bullshit."

Waiting to see if she had any more to say, Patrick asks something that I never thought he would. "What about your writing? Have you even thought about sitting down to write this whole time you were hiding under the covers?"

"No," I say with part shame and part wondering why I hadn't.

"The girls told me that you lost your manuscripts in the fire, but really, who cares? You were always starting things and putting them aside because you hated them. I can remember you working on a couple of stories when we were together. All of which wound up in the…what did you call it again…the maybe later pile. And need I remind you about the one with the vampire in it? I believe that that particular gem was started when we were dating. Not sure how far you got in that one."

"Stop. Stop it right there. I have enough to deal with. We don't need to relive that particular moment in my attempt to enter the world of the supernatural."

"I don't know. I think that some of us might want to know about that one," Bobby says with a devilish smirk.

"What I am saying is that you didn't find your voice with any of those other stories, so why not start a new one. The fire is a blessing. You have no choice but to move forward." Patrick gets up and starts walking over to me. "This is why I am here. You need to start writing. You need to stop whatever this is and write. Once you do, then we can talk again."

When did Patrick Lord become this invested in my life?

"And here. Maybe this will help you get there." He hands me a yellow envelope and walks out of the apartment.

After Patrick left, I have to endure about three more hours of my friends telling me how I'm not myself and that I need to stop all of my self-pity. Some of it I listen to, but most of it I tune out as I stare out the window at my city. When had New York become something that I feared and hid from?

As I stand up, I look at all the faces staring back at me. My eyes rest on my aunt. She has been quiet this whole time, just observing. I know that she has a lot to say, but I also know she will not be saying it now. I weakly smile and she holds up her glass as if to cheers. You have to love a woman who drinks a dirty martini at eleven o'clock in the morning.

"Thank you all for this." Without anything further said, I grab the yellow envelope and walk down the hall into my bedroom. With a click of the door I am alone.

Even in the darkness of this curtained room, I see it all. I see mounds of clothes and piles of papers with books thrown around scattered on the floor. I see the pain of losing my home and the security that I had felt within those four walls. I see the disappointment of being fired for standing up for myself. I see the stupidity of thinking that I can control everything in my life. There are things you just can't predict. More importantly, I see that I let myself give into it all.

There is a soft knock at the door before it starts to open. "Cami?" It is my Aunt JoJo. I run into her arms and start to cry.

She slowly pulls away from me while walking toward the curtains. In one quick movement, she flings open the curtains and takes a look around. "Well, this just will not do."

"Aunt Jo…"

"Look around? This place looks like a frat house. Not that I would have much experience being in one of those," she says with a side glance and a smirk.

"Oh, I am sure." Leave it to my aunt to try and make light of the situation.

"Sophia is right. This place needs to be cleaned. May I suggest a hazmat team?"

"Very funny. It is not that bad." It sort of is.

"Oh, my dear. You listen to me. I know you have been through it today. I was skeptical when Sophia called me about this whole intervention thing, but I think that this was good for you. I know that you are tired of people telling you what you need to do and all their feelings about the way you have been coping, so I am going to make this quick." With a deep breath and channeling all the bravado she can, she yells, "Snap out of it!"

And then she is gone with her blonde curls swinging from side to side as she walks down the hallway. That was all she had for me. Four words that shocked me and stung a little too. Out of everything I heard today, that hit me more than everything else. Sophia's plea pulled at my heart strings, but my aunt knew that when she said this, it would bring me back to a different place in my head.

I used to spend countless Saturday nights when I was younger watching movies at Aunt JoJo's Tribeca apartment as my parents went to their events. Then, as I got older, I used her home as a much needed escape from the Upper East Side drama. Our favorite movie was *Moonstruck*. I love the dynamic of the characters and Cher is just perfection. However, the moment I love the most is when Ronny tells Loretta that he is in love with her after just meeting and sleeping together. Her response? Two smacks and a *snap out of it*. Somehow, JoJo knew that with those words, I would remember what I am doing now is not who I am. I guess I should be glad she left out the smack across the face.

Taking stock in what is around me, I notice the yellow envelope that Patrick handed to me laying on my bed. I grab for it and undo the metal clasp at the top. Inside are typed pages with notes all over them. On more careful inspection, I can see that they are my typed pages, but I lost this manuscript in the fire. *How?*

Since there is no way that I can do anything until I clean up, I shove the papers back in the envelope and place it over by my laptop. I take the first small step. I grab my dirty clothes and head down to the laundry room. *Small steps, Cami.*

Chapter Fourteen

THREE MONTHS AGO, I WAS SITTING IN MY BED-room separating myself from everyone else while I spent hours clicking the refresh button on my email every two minutes, praying for a response to my resume. I was living within four walls and allowing my mind to go to the darkest places of self-pity. That pity party I was having broke away piece by piece the person who I was. Now, I am working on realizing that I am enough for those around me and that I don't have to be in control all the time. I have even come up with a mantra that has replaced my ten-year plan. *Shit happens. It is how you deal with it that makes you stronger and creates the path to who you are supposed to be.* I may even laminate that.

❧

Waiting for Sophia in a corner cafe, I stare at my phone, waiting to hear back from an editor of a magazine that I submitted a short story to. Though I still have my moments when I want to drink wine from the bottle with a straw, I am getting better. I shower more regularly and my organizational skills are back to being utilized. I got a desk organizer with a new set of fancy file folders for my desk. I even moved out of Sophia's townhouse. It pained me to dip into my inheritance for the apartment and for monthly expenses, but I needed to have my own space. I love the place that I got in Chelsea and am slowly making it home. A very small home with no closet space, but mine nonetheless.

"I love the fall!" Sophia exclaims as she plops in the seat across from me.

"I know. Long live pumpkin spice!" I hold up my coffee cup and take a sip.

"It is so nice out that I might even take my sketch-book to the park."

"Really? You haven't done that in years. What has gotten into you? You seem…"

"Happy?"

"No. That cannot be it."

"Well. I am. So there. Waitress, when you have a minute?" Sophia gave her order and continued. "I am *actually* happy. The art is going well. I have officially put the townhouse on the market. And ..."

"And what?"

"And I am seeing someone."

"You are always seeing *someone*. I don't think that you have ever been not seeing someone."

"Don't hate on me just because you haven't gotten laid since the first time Obama was sworn into office."

"Ouch. True, but still." I take another sip of coffee and as the waitress brings over a stack of pumpkin ginger pancakes I pre-ordered for both of us.

"It is *very* new, but this time it feels different."

"Different, huh? I have to hear this."

"His name is William. He is a screenplay writer that I met at my last opening. We have a lot in common."

"Such as?" I say with a mouth full of pancakes.

"Attractive, Cam. And you wonder why you don't have a man in your life."

"I don't wonder. I know. Now, what about all these many things you have in common with Billy Boy."

"For starters, we both have asshole friends that bust our chops all the time." She says with a smile. I make a kiss face as she continues. "We both love art and walking around museums. He actually reads newspapers. Like, real paper newspapers. He is smart. Not only book smart, but real-life experiences intelligence. We never struggle for something to talk about. It is just easy with him. And then there is the parents' thing."

"What parents' thing?"

"He lost his father a couple of years ago from a heart attack. He was the rock of their family and took care of everything for his mom. Because it was so sudden, his death left them with a lot to deal with emotionally and financially. So, he gets what it is like for me around the holidays or on my parents' birthdays. Will gets that sometimes I just need to have a dark day where I spend time alone with my thoughts."

"I am really happy for you, Soph."

"So how about you? Anything new with the writing? Dating anyone?" She says fishing for any tidbit that she can.

"Nothing much. I connected with a few publishers that have given me some freelance editing gigs. I haven't heard much else in terms of the job front. It is difficult out there. It seems that no matter what I apply for there is someone younger or more desperate who is willing to do it for half the pay." Taking a pause, I notice that Sophia is hoovering her pancakes. *She must be working up quite the appetite with Will.* "I started to write again too. I am easing myself into it with some short stories that I have sent out to handful of magazines. I don't think that anything will happen with that."

"Wait. When did this happen? You wrote something and I haven't read it yet?"

"It is just a quick story. I haven't been able to do much more than that, but my ability to stare at a blank screen has become almost perfected. What can I say? The voices in my head just aren't talking to me."

"For once."

"Hey!"

"So I was thinking that we all should go out tonight. Nothing crazy, but there is a bar called the O'Leary's that Will always goes to on game night. We thought it might be fun to invite everyone."

"Oh, *we* thought it would be a good idea? You are a we now? I never thought I would see the day!"

"Shut it. Are you up for it or do you need to organize your underwear drawer?" Sophia puts a stack of cash under the bill and begins to get up.

"Count me in." Standing up, I smooth out my coat. "Now what type of game will we be watching?"

"Rugby. And we are cheering for the Irish team."

"Oh dear Lord. Does Bobby know this?"

"Yes. He's seeing if he can find a shirt with a lion on it."

"A lion?"

"Spain's rugby team is nicknamed Los Leones."

"Got it. Are they playing the Irish team?"

"I have no idea."

"This should be interesting," I say shaking my head. "What can I say?"

"That, basically, Bobby is planning on getting the crap knocked out of him."

"He has balls. I will give him that."

"That he does. Hey. Check this out." I point in a window of an office building. "Coming Soon…Patty Publishing. Have you ever heard of them?"

"Um. Cam. When was the last time you talked to Patrick?"

"Three months ago. Why?"

"I think that you should talk to him."

"Again. Why?"

"Patty Publishing is Patrick's company."

"Wow. He really did it."

"Yeah. I think you should talk to him."

"Yeah…" I say as we walk away from the construction site.

൭൭

Margo, Paula, Jenny, and I walk into O'Leary's Bar that night. I am expecting a few people sitting around watching a game. What I get is a packed house of rowdy men screaming at the wall of TVs and sloshing beer all over the place.

"Well, this is…" Margo says from behind me searching for a word. "Authentic."

"So this is where all the hot Irish men have been

hiding." Jenny looks around as if her brain is going into overload.

"And look at him." Paula points to the bartender while she squeezes up next to me.

"Who?" Margo's interest is piqued.

"The bartender. Doesn't he look familiar?"

"I don't know, but I am willing to find out." Jenny pushes us all out of the way as she makes her way through the crowd to the bar.

"And I am going to need a drink if I am going to make it through this night," I say, following her.

As the rest of us make it to the bar, Jenny is chatting up the bartender as she orders the other girls' drinks. Through this mess of people, I can see his eyes drift over to me. They are the color of a cerulean blue sky and they are staring right at me. For the first time in a long time, my knees go weak. I think I recognize him, but for the life of me I don't know where. I know that stare from somewhere.

As I walk up to the bar, he turns and says with a slight accent, "What can I get you?"

"Bourbon on the rocks."

"Finally. Someone who doesn't want something pink, with a twist of lime or a rim of salt on the glass." He reaches up to grab a bottle of Knob Creek.

"K.I.S.S."

"Alright." He leans over the bar and kisses my cheek.

"Not a kiss. K.I.S.S. Keep it simple, stupid. When

dealing with drinks at a bar I keep it as simple as possible. It is either bourbon or red wine."

"Got ya. That makes sense, but you can't take back the kiss." He gives an exaggerated wink. "So what brings you to this fine establishment tonight?"

"Apparently, I am here for some sort of match thingy."

"Match *thingy*. You did not just say that."

"What?" I try to look as Pollyannaish as possible.

"It is rugby. It makes your football look like a bunch of kindergarteners playing capture the flag. It combines all three of the S's."

"The three S's?"

"Speed. Strength. Strategy."

"And here I was thinking that it was just an excuse for a bunch of hot men in shorts to run around, tackle each other, and play with their balls."

"A smart ass. Tell me you are part Irish and we will set the date."

"Nope. I don't have any Irish in me." And as soon as the words come out, I can't believe that I set myself up for that one. *Please don't be that guy that uses a line like that. Please. Please. Please. You are too cute for that. Please.*

"Sorry to hear that…" He waits as if I am supposed to finish the sentence.

"He wants your name." A waitress in skin-tight jeans and black tank-top, showing off her full sleeve of tattoos on her left arm, comes up behind him. "Jake here is trying to be smooth, but as usual is failing miserably."

"Siobhan. Why are you over here?"

"Beer for table five and shots for the bimbos at table two. So, your name?" the waitress asks while turning toward me, growing visibly more impatient.

"Camilla. But my friends call me Cami."

"And there we have it. He is Jake. You are Camilla. I on the other hand still need a pitcher of beer and two shots of tequila."

"Coming right up." He turns to the tap to fill her order. As he places the last shot on her tray she mockingly curtseys toward him.

"Now. Where were we?"

"I too am still waiting for my drink."

"Right. Sorry about that." He looks around as if he doesn't know where anything is as he puts his hand on the back of his neck.

For a minute I almost lose my train of thought as I stare at his arms. *Damn.* His shirt is pulling in all the right areas showing off an impressive tattoo on his arm. He must spend a lot of time lifting liquor boxes to have muscles like that. *I am screwed.* Trying to regain my composure, I manage to get out, "You seem a little flustered. Exactly how long have you been a bartender?"

"Me?"

"Is there anyone else back there with you? Wait. If there is I don't want to know."

"I am not."

"Not what?"

"I am not a bartender."

"The fact that you are standing behind the bar giving people drinks might be giving off the wrong impression then."

"I am filling in for my dad. He owns the bar, but had to stay home to take care of my mom. She twisted her ankle when she was trying to clean the top shelf of liquor over there." He points behind him as he finished up my drink order. "Bourbon on the rocks."

"Thanks." I quickly take a much needed sip. Then I notice a girl is giving me the stink eye from down the bar. "Um. I think you have a fan over there." I point to the woman who is sitting up straight so that her boobs are pushed out. When he looks her way, I turn toward the girls who I had completely forgotten and are standing behind me.

"What was that?" Margo says.

"What was what?" I say innocently as I look around for Sophia and Will.

"Were you flirting with that bartender?" Jenny asks.

"I wasn't flirting."

"Like hell you weren't. Cami is getting her groove back." Sophia comes up behind me as she starts doing the running man. She is obviously a few more drinks into the night than we are.

Grabbing her shoulders with my free hand, I look her in the eyes. "You need to never do that in public again. And if you do, make sure that I have my phone out because that shit is going viral."

"Sooooo. Where is this William that we keep hearing about?" Margo links her arm into Sophia's.

"Right over here with Bobby."

"No way." Margo stops dead in her tracks. "You are dating him? He is what? Sixty? Seventy?"

"He is fifty."

"No way. With all the guys you have dated—and there have been a lot—I never could have seen this one coming." Margo states.

"Okay. This is going to become nasty in a minute, so let's all just shelve the comments and play nice." Paula separates the two and leads Margo away as I try to calm Sophia down.

"Why didn't you tell me he was older?" I ask.

"Because I don't really see him that way. I have dated the artists, the bad boys, the so-called intellectuals, the film makers, the Wall Street captains of industry, and the wanna-be real estate moguls. All of them have been around our age and they are immature butt heads."

"Valid point. Continue."

"William is smart, funny, and he just wants to be with me. I didn't have to wonder if he was dating other women because after the first couple of weeks we had *the talk*."

"The talk?"

"I keep forgetting you are a commitment phobe. We had the exclusivity talk where we both said that we would only be seeing each other. He is a grown-ass man and I don't need to validate my relationship to her."

Sophia points to Margo who is now introducing herself to William.

"Correct. You don't have to explain yourself to anyone, but you know Margo. She is always the one that makes quick judgments and then recants them later. I am sure that she will apologize before the night is over for being so bitchy."

"She better."

"Now. Why don't we head on over there? We have left your boyfriend with all three of them…alone."

"Crap." Sophia almost does a Flo Jo across the bar before Paula can start asking what his FICO score is and Jenny winds up sitting in his lap.

As I predicted, everyone loves William. Margo bought a round of drinks as her 'I am sorry I stuck my foot in my mouth' apology. He is teaching us about rugby, but the basic theme of the evening is when everyone else cheers, you cheer. So, I cheer and then I drink. Then I rinse and repeat. At this point, I have a healthy buzz on and am feeling pretty good. As I look around the table, I see Sophia. She is beaming. I have never seen Sophia so giddy while out with a guy before. She is laughing, touching his arm, and sneaking quick kisses. This is a complete one-eighty from her usual no public displays of affection clause in her other relationships. *She is finally happy.*

When it is time to take a trip to the bathroom, Paula stays back to talk to Bobby and William. While Jenny is on the prowl for a single Irishman to have a little fun with, Margo, Sophia, and I make our way down a darkened hallway only to be greeted with two doors. One marked Fir and the other Mná.

"What the… How drunk am I right now?" Margo says as she gets ridiculously close to the two signs.

"I don't know, but am I the only one that doesn't think those are real words?" Sophia adds while tilting her head to one side.

"Okay. We are mildly drunk, educated women. We can figure this out. I have my phone. Hold on," I add just as a woman came out of the door labeled Mná.

"Or we just use this one." Sophia walks in.

On our way out and back down the hallway, I hear my phone from inside my purse. "You guys go ahead. I want to answer this. Hello?"

"Camilla."

"Hello? I can barely hear you." A roar of the crowd bellows down the corridor and my phone goes dead. "Damn it!" I smack my phone into my palm as if that is going to make the call come back.

Next thing I know, my heel is caught in the floorboard and I hear a crack. My ankle twists to the right as I reach out for the wall to try and maintain my balance. *Seriously? What the… No!* I bend my leg to see the bottom of the shoe and heel is just hanging there. It is flapping in the breeze, mocking me for spending too much on these red-bottomed beauties. As I try to hobble back into the bar, my ankle gives out on me and I start to stumble again. Then I can feel an arm wrap around my waist and pull me up. As I am turned around, pushed into the most muscular chest I have ever had against me. *Damn.*

"You should be more careful."

"What I should have done is not wear my good Louboutin's to a sports bar with a craptastic floor." My eyes adjust to the dim lighting to see the same piercing blue eyes that I was swooning over hours before. Being this close to him allows me to see him even better than when he was behind the bar. From his slightly messy dark chocolate colored hair to his chiseled jaw to a mouth that just begs to be kissed, this man is a perfect mix of Henry Cavill, Charlie Hunnam, and Chris Pine. *Get it together, Cami.*

"Don't blame it on the floor. You shouldn't have been assaulting your phone and not looking where you were walking. And would it kill you to say thank you for stopping you from falling on your ass right now?"

"Sorry. Thank you. I am just pissed. These were good shoes." I hold up the stiletto. "And shoes are not supposed to double as ventriloquist dummies." I move the heel and bottom of the shoe to mimic a Pac-Man type mouth.

"Can you move?" He says as he carefully leans me up against the wall and steps back.

"You can let me go. I will be alright now." The pain in my ankle is throbbing, but I can't stay here forever.

"Are you sure?" The concern in his voice is way more comforting than it should be for someone I just met hours before.

"Yes. I will be okay. I promise."

Pulling away slowly, I am able to get a closer look at his elaborate tattoo. It is an anchor with nautical designs moving up his forearm. *At one point, you will lose your footing in a distracted moment. Fear not. This will allow you to find your mainstay.* The statement pops into my head and just as quickly leaves.

"Why don't you come back to the office? My sister keeps an extra couple pair of flats back there. Not sure what size you are or if they will fit."

"You don't have to do that."

"Do what?"

"You don't owe me anything, least of all a pair of shoes." I say. "Though… I suppose it was your family bar's floor that killed my stilettos."

"Right this way." He leads me down the hallway with his arm around my waist until we get to a cramped office. Looking around, he picks up a canvas tote bag that is on the floor in the corner. "Here. Pick one of these." He dangles one option from either hand.

I grab the black pair and manage to wedge my foot in. Cinderella, I am not.

"Thanks for this," I say as I stare at his chiseled jaw and then move down to his arms.

"What? Do I have something on me?"

"Nice ink." I point to his arm trying to deflect the fact that I was just blatantly ogling him.

"This? It was my first."

"It is beautiful. The lines and the shading are really well done."

"Are you an artist or something?"

"No. My best friend is. I am a …"

"You are a…"

"I am a writer," I say with way more confidence that I expect.

"Any I might have read?"

"Not yet. I was an editor for a bunch of years which didn't end so well. Now, I am trying to not think about my path in life. I am being guided by my dreams."

"How very enlightened of you."

"Isn't it though? I was thinking about putting it on a t-shirt. You should have seen me last summer. Enlightened would have not been the word that I would have used to describe myself." *Why am I telling him this?*

"And what would you have said?"

"I was a hot mess in a black hole of pity." *Keep going, Cami. You will have him running out of the room in no time.*

"Ah. The artist's crisis. Something goes the wrong way and you are sent down a spiral of why everyone else and I suck."

"Exactly. So, tell me, not-a-bartender Jake. How is it that you understand the existential crisis of the artist so well?"

"I am an actor."

"Ah," I say.

"What is that supposed to mean?"

"I would have guessed model, but actor fits too. You are…well have you looked at yourself in the mirror? It would be a shame if you weren't doing something that shared all of that with the female population." *What am I saying? This is why I should never drink and talk to hot guys.*

"Are you saying that you think I am good-looking?" he says mockingly as his hand went to his chest.

"Don't look so shocked. I think that ninety percent of the women and possibly a few of the men in this bar think you are hot."

"So now I am hot," he says with a smile.

My heart beats faster as he gets closer. "Well. I mean. You're going to make me say it, aren't you?"

"Yes."

"Ugh. Fine. You are hot."

"Now was that so difficult?"

"No. I suppose not."

"So now that we established you think I am good looking, how about you give me your number? Maybe grab some coffee or dinner some time?"

"You're an actor."

"So. You're a writer. There we have both stated our professions for the second time. Now what?"

"Well, for me, being an actor is a deal breaker no matter how hot a guy is." I look around trying to see if I can put any space between us. With the amount of alcohol, I have in my system, and the sexiness that is wafting off this man, I don't know how much longer I will be able to not jump him.

"Wait. Wait. Let me get this straight. Because I am an actor, you can't date me."

"Yes."

"Why?"

"Why?"

"That is the question that I just asked."

"It is stupid and you will not understand."

"Just try me."

"Fine. I have a list of professions that I will under no circumstances date. Actor, musician, professional athlete, journalist, and farmer are the top five."

"Farmer?"

"Yeah…never going to happen. I am a city girl. I don't even go camping unless it is *Troop Beverly Hills* style."

"And is there a reason for this aversion to acting?"

"It is just that I wouldn't want to see the guy I am with getting all hot and heavy with some other woman on a big screen or on stage. I know it isn't cheating, but still you have to tap into some emotions to be a character and I think it would be naive to think that those residual feelings just disappear as soon as you hear 'cut'."

"Ah. I see."

"So alas, we are not meant to be."

"What if I say that I am not an actor?"

"But you are."

"Well. Right now. I am spending my days and nights bartending here for a while. So…"

"Technically, you are bartender."

"What do you say? Are you willing to go out with a bartender?"

"You are serious?"

"Absofuckinglutely. Now give me your phone."

"I don't know about this." As soon as the words are out of my mouth, I know that I am going to give him my phone. Isn't this what I am supposed to be doing. *Live a little Cami.*

"Hand it over."

"Fine. Here." I unlock the screen and shove the phone in his hand.

With a couple of swipes and a lot of clicking with his thumbs, he looks up at me with an almost evil smile. He pulls me close to him and snaps a shot before I am ready. "Perfect. Let me just text myself. There. Good to go."

He hands me back my phone and I take a moment to look at the photo of us. *We look good together.* I shake my head and moving on from the thought that I just had. "So now I have your number. What exactly am I supposed to do with this?"

"Answer it when I call you," he whispers in my ear as he brushes past me. "I think we should head back out there. I don't want your friends thinking anything torrid is happening back here."

We make our way back into the main bar area when I see that Bobby was coming right for me. When I turn to say goodbye to Jake, he is gone.

"Who were you just talking to?"

"Jake."

"Holy shit. Ho-ly shit." Bobby keeps shaking his head back and forth. "You. Him. You and him."

"What's going on?" Jenny comes up behind us.

"Our friend Cami just hooked up with the next heartthrob panty dropper coming to a theater near you." Bobby says as he continues to shake his head in disbelief.

"Whoa. Slow your roll. I did not hook up with or do anything with that man other than talk to him. I fell and he gave me his sister's shoes. End of story." I hold up my broken shoe as I sit down at our table.

"No! Your poor shoe." Margo looks generally disturbed by the sight of the deconstructed heel.

"Forget the shoe. This could be a huge scoop in the gossip world. I am going to have to hand in my man card for a moment, but let's talk about that guy." Bobby points to Jake standing at the bar. "You were just talking to *the* Jacob O'Leary. He has been slated to play a lead character superhero in the next DC Comics summer blockbuster."

"Holy shit," Everyone says in unison.

Walking over to the table with a wine glass and a bottle of IPA, Will takes his seat next to Sophia. "So Jake says that you two had a fun talk."

"You know Jake?" Bobby turns to face Will.

"Of course. It is why I come to this bar. We worked together on an indie in New York a couple of years ago. We used the bar in some of the scenes. The film got nominated for a Golden Globe, but it was really Jake that everyone was talking about. I found out that he grew up in Ireland where his family owned some sort of whiskey company. Then his parents and him moved to New York and opened this bar. I love coming here on the off chance that I will run into him. He is a great sounding board for new ideas."

"So you knew who he was and didn't tell us?" Sophia smacks his arm.

"He really isn't the type of guy that likes people to know who he is. When he is not on set, Jake is just a normal guy. Somehow, the fame just doesn't go to his head." Will takes a sip of his beer. "Look at him. None of you knew who he really is. To most people he is just the hot bartender that reminds them of someone. He blends in well."

"Yeah. He blends," I say as I down the last drops of my drink.

Looking back at the bar, I see Jake laugh with someone. There is something about him. It scares me that a man I just met could stir up emotions that I have not felt for a while. I am drawn to him in a way that is more than sexually. I can't put my finger on it.

It is important that during difficult times you open your heart.

Later that night, I sit on the edge of my bed, looking at the photo of Jake and I. The two smiling faces staring back at me are mocking me with their merriment. Am I really going to stick by the dating list of do's and don'ts? After everything that has happened and is happening to me now, why am I clinging to this ideal? It has done squat for me in the past. Maybe for once, I should just take the leap of faith and pray that he will not hurt me.

He is not Joseph.

Chapter Fifteen

THE NEXT MORNING, AFTER POURING MY COFFEE, I sit down to check my emails. It is my ritual. Though I know that I should step back, I have to see what is waiting for me. I don't know what I expect, but there is always that one moment when I am signing in that I think…maybe. Maybe someone will respond to a resume I sent out months ago. Maybe an editor is getting back to me about the short story. Just…Maybe.

To try to reduce some of my stress, last week I decided that I am not going to apply for any more full-time jobs for a few months. The truth is, I am not getting the responses I want and it is starting to piss me off. When I get pissed off, I stress and start to spiral down into a headspace that I just don't want to get into again. Been there. Done that.

If this were last summer, I would be running through all the ways that I have failed my parents, my grandparents, and myself by not being able to get a job. These toxic thoughts still bounce around in my brain, but I do my best not to let them creep in and stay longer than a moment. It is a constant battle to have these days that I can't help but feel a little less than everyone else, but I just keep telling myself that I am stronger than this. I'm a New Yorker, damn it.

Scanning through the junk and the few random links with cats and dogs doing weird things that Sophia likes to send me, I nearly drop my cup. There is an email from Ethel from *Exhibition*'s Human Resources Department entitled KARMA. I have not heard from the magazine or Ethel since the week after my firing when she sent me an email telling me that my employment record would not reflect what Joel claimed. Apparently, the accusations could not be backed up so they were not included in the termination statement. I still had to deal with the fact that I was fired, but at least there were no comments about my paying people to do my work for me. *What a prick.*

Since being fired and Bobby leaving the publication, I fell out of touch with what was going on there. Though, being in the circle we were, rumors are always floating about. I heard through some mutual friends that there was a lot of turmoil at the company. *Exhibition* has been relegated to bottom of the online news food chain because of the onslaught of newbies with amazing writers who have a much larger following and social media presence.

There is also still a buzz about how Sal unceremoniously kicked his son to the curb after finding a large amount of funds being transferred to a personal account in Joel's name. Employees thought it was the lack of advertising that was causing the delay in payroll. Yeah... not so much.

Now, my hand hovering over the mouse, I wonder what this is all about. With two clicks, I am on YouTube staring at a video called MERV THE PERVE GETS HIS. As it begins to play, I notice it is at a club that opened six months ago. There is a group of women sitting at the bar as Joel walks up to them. He leans over and says something to a busty redhead. Next thing you know she slaps him across the face and pours a drink on him. He grabs her hand and attempts to drag her across the club. However, this woman wasn't having it. She manages to get free and quickly goes back to her friends who are now talking to one of the bouncers. You can see the anger on Joel's face. The scene fades to black and then you are in the *Exhibition* offices with Joel leaning over a cubicle talking to a female employee. As the videographer zooms in, you can hear that he is making advances to the girl sitting at my old desk. She is visibly upset, but tries to ignore him. Scene after scene shows Joel hitting on women, making inappropriate jokes about them, or touching them in every setting imaginable. The person who took this video followed him to the gym, in the park, at work, at charity events, and out around town with his friends. I can't believe what I am watching and then it happens. Pausing the video, I can see that the woman from the beginning scene at the club is in the *Exhibition* offices flashing an NYPD badge. *The same woman! Now that is just perfect.* She and her partner go into Joel's office. Next thing you know, Joel is handcuffed and all three of them are walking in front of all the staff to the elevator as the detectives mirandize him. He tries to push away the person taking the video with his shoulder, but loses his balance and falls flat on his face. This part has been replayed a few times as a catchy tune plays in the background. At the end of the video, Joel's mug shot shows up on the screen and a list of his offenses, including embezzlement, is listed like the end credits of a movie. The video has over two million hits and counting.

Thank you, Ethel.

After delighting in the video of Joel, I don't think that this day could get any better. I signed off my email, topped off my coffee, and sat down to write. Three hours later, I have two paragraphs that I have rewritten fifteen times. I need a break, so I decide to check my emails to see if Margo emailed me about my social media tutorial. She has been after me to start to get more active on the accounts she set up for me a month ago. And then I see it. It is an email from the magazine that I submitted my article to. Taking a deep breath and praying that this is good news, I start to read.

> Dear Ms. Valentini,
>
> Thank you for your submission. We regret to inform you that we will not be accepting your short story for the next issue. However, ...

There is a however. I start to wiggle in my seat.

> However, our senior editors liked the style of your writing and your overall voice. We were wondering if you would like to come in for an interview to explore the possibility of having you write a web series and/or a column for the print magazine.
>
> Please email me back with your availability.
>
> Sincerely,
> Katrina Smeedly

I re-read the email six times before I take a screen-shot and send it to Sophia. I need to know that this is in fact happening. I am actually getting a response back from a major magazine. They want to talk to me about writing for them. I cannot believe this. Yet somewhere in the back of my head, I can't help thinking, what if I fail?

Pushing down the doubt, my phone rings, but I have no idea where it is. Following the noise, I find it underneath my pillow. Without looking at who it is, I pick it up and scream into the mouthpiece. "Squeeeee! Can you believe it?"

"Damn." I hear a low mumble.

"Soph?"

"Who? This is Jake."

"Jake? Jake who?"

"Well, I see that I made quite the impression on you last night."

"Oh. Sorry. Um. I am just a little all over the place this morning."

"That's alright. How about dinner tonight?"

"I don't know. I have plans with some—"

"You're going to blow me off with that I have plans with the girls line?"

"Actually, I was going to blow you off with the I have plans with my Aunt line."

"Well, then. What about coffee?"

"I don't think that this is a good idea."

"Are you still hung up on the whole actor thing?"

"Yes. No. I don't know." I take a deep breath. "Why are you pushing this? There has to be a million other women that you can be harassing right now. What is your end game?"

"Wow. That is harsh. Why can't I just want to hang out with you?"

"Because in my experience, guys just don't want to hang out with women who turn them down. What is it, two times now?"

"I don't think that we need to put a number on it. However, technically this is the first time you are turning me down. Last night, you sort of caved."

"I did not cave."

"Whatever you say. I liked talking to you last night and thought that we could continue the conversation today. I am leaving for California in two weeks, so I don't want to waste time not getting to know you."

"I don't know how I feel about this."

"I am just a guy on the other end of the phone asking a girl to get coffee with me."

"You did not just hijack a Julia Roberts line right now."

"What can I say? I love me some *Notting Hill*."

Laughing, I manage to get out, "Fine. What is the chance that you are going to let this go?"

"The odds are not in your favor. I will keep calling until you say that you will meet me at least once. Meet me at Bryant Park at three. Sound good?"

"Just one coffee and then you will leave me alone."

"Sure. But after one afternoon with me, you won't want to be alone."

"Oh brother. What am I getting myself into?"

A loud sound of bottles breaking echoed through his phone. "Shit. I have to go, but see you at three."

This should be interesting. Plopping into my love seat, I find myself excited about meeting up with him. It is just coffee, but the idea of starting something new with Jake is invigorating.

As thoughts of Jake start to fill my head, I remember the email. I immediately jump up and run back over to my computer. I have to respond to Katrina. This could be the big break that I need. In a few keystrokes, I give her a couple of dates and times that I would be able to come in. I don't want to seem too eager, even though I am practically bouncing up and down on my chair as I respond.

With that sent, I turn to my closet. *What the hell am I going to wear?*

❧

Standing in Bryant Park, I arrived fifteen minutes earlier than I should have. It is a crisp fall day, so choosing my camel-colored wool cardigan layered with a purple shirt under it, skinny jeans, and knee-high brown leather boots was perfect. My hair was pin straight which gives the appearance of not trying too hard, but in reality, takes

me over an hour to get it that way because of my naturally curly hair. All in all, I think that I am looking how
I should to meet a friend for coffee. The thing is, I have
butterflies in my stomach and I am sort of freaking out.

This is not a date, I keep telling myself over and over
until I see him. I don't think he sees me yet, so I have a
moment to bask in the fact that this man looks this good
in his faded jeans and leather jacket. All of my resolve to
not fall for this guy is fading away.

*Calm down. You have known him for less than a day.
Sure, he looks like sex on a stick, but he has flaws. He has to
have flaws. Just think about something else. Anything else.
Global warming. Forest fires. Politics. Waking up next to
him and that smile. Damn it.*

"Hey." Jake approaches with his hands in his pockets
as I am talking to myself.

"Hey. You look…" I stare at him for a moment and
something seems off. "Are you alright?"

"I just got some news about my mom, but let's not
talk about that. How about some coffee?" He starts
walking toward COFFEED. "Why don't you grab a spot
to sit and I will get us a few things? What do you want?
Some sort of latte thing?"

"Coffee. Black."

"How did I not guess that a girl who orders bourbon
on the rocks would have her coffee black?"

"I am an enigma."

"Wrapped in a riddle?"

"Exactly." I eye the table about ten feet away and gesture that I am going to be over there. He turns and waits in line to place our order.

As he sits down, Jake places the coffees on the table along with the most amazing looking cookies. "I hope you don't expect to get any of these."

I quickly grab one and break off a piece.

"Hungry?" He asks with a hint of laughter as he watches me eat.

"For cookies. Always. This place has some really tasty baked goods."

"Tasty baked goods?"

"What?" I shove another cookie bite into my mouth.

"Nothing. I like a girl who eats."

"Well then you are out with the right person."

"There is something about you Cami that I can't put my finger on. You have this way about you. Plus, you don't seem to care about what I think of you. I like it."

"Oh. You mean that I don't fawn all over you or kiss your soon-to-be superhero ass?"

With a cringe, he says, "You heard about that? I was hoping to string you along with the whole struggling artist thing. Maybe get you to cave and agree to go out with me on another date."

"You said I just had to have coffee with you and then that was it."

"Correct. But let's face it. We are going to have another date."

"Nope. I think that I am good with this." I am not letting him get the upper hand on this one.

"We will have to see about that," he says as he takes a sip of his coffee. "You are exhausting. Has anyone ever told you that?"

"Once or twice. I prefer to be called stubborn though, for future reference."

"Duly noted." he looks around and let out a huge sigh.

"So. What is going on with your mom?"

"We don't have to talk about that."

"I can tell something is going on. And I get it. We have only known each other for less than a day, but I am a good listener. Especially when I am caffeinated and fed."

He takes a minute to just look at me as if assessing whether or not to talk to a relative stranger about his family problems. "Do you remember when I mentioned that my mom fell at the bar?"

"That's why you were filling in, right?"

"Yup." He runs his fingers in his hair. "When my mom fell at the bar, she had to be brought to the hospital. They did a bunch of tests and said that everything was fine. She just sprained her ankle and would have to keep off of it for a while."

"That makes sense."

"Yeah. Then this morning her doctor called. He said he took a look at her X-rays they sent him and something didn't seem right."

"What the hell is that supposed to mean?"

"That is what I said. Apparently, they had a mix-up in the ER that night and my mom's X-rays got switched with someone else's. There was a lot of commotion that day because of a car accident that came in at the same time as us. So now she has to stay off of her leg until we can get her back to take more tests. My sister is running around like my mom has a disease and my father keeps bitching that he will have to take over more of her shifts and responsibilities at the bar. Then you can add into the mix that I have to leave in two weeks to start filming."

"And you are concerned that it is something serious?"

"No. I think it is just a pain in the ass, but my family takes even the most normal situations and elevates them to a catastrophe. Plus, my mom doesn't exactly believe what doctors tell her, so I keep catching her doing stuff she shouldn't be."

"Like what?"

"This morning she was trying to climb a ladder with one leg."

"No. She didn't."

"I swear. I didn't know if I should laugh or scream. There she was a sixty-year-old woman trying to change a lightbulb on a ladder with her foot bandaged up, wincing in pain. They are all going to be the death of me."

"Okay. I have an idea." I stand up and grab his empty coffee cup. "We are going to take your mind off of all of this."

"What do you have in mind?" he asks a little too eagerly.

"You will see." I grab his hand and hail a cab.

Entering the doors of The Strand, the smell of books welcomes me. Out of every place in New York that I take refuge in, this is one that never disappoints.

"You are taking me to a bookstore."

"This is not just a bookstore. This is The Strand. It is an institution."

"A bookstore."

"If you cannot recognize the awesomeness of this establishment, then let's go." I turn around to walk back out the door in my best angry toddler impression. Just then, Jake puts his arms around me and walks us further into the store.

"Okay. Show me the magic."

I don't think I have ever had so much fun in a bookstore before. Shelf after shelf, I show Jake countless books that have influenced my life. We talk about growing up in New York, our careers, and what the past year of my life has been like. I have to give him credit for not running out the door screaming.

Jake really starts to get into it when he finds a few Ian Fleming novels and a selection of pulp fiction classics. By the end of our trip, we are laughing about the most random things while carrying out an impressive haul of books. It is getting late and Jake is going to fill in at the bar again. I have to get over to Sophia's to help in packing, so we decide to part ways. He lingers a bit too long as I stand at the door of my cab. *Is he going to kiss me? Do I want him to kiss me?*

"Thanks for today," he says.

"No problem."

"You know that I want to see you again."

"I know that." And God help me, I want to see him too.

"But you deserve more. You have been through a lot this past year and I don't want to be another thing added to the list. I am gone in…"

"I get it." And with that he kisses me on the cheek and starts to walk away down the street. Turning to the cabbie, I say, "Hold on a minute."

"Miss. You cannot…"

"Just start the meter. I will pay for the time." That shuts him up real quick.

I start to run down the street when I see that he is standing on the corner waiting for the light to turn. "Jake!" I scream, and fifty people turn to look at me with annoyance.

I cannot believe I am doing this.

"Jake."

He is facing me with the most confused look on his face and then he smiles. I put my arms around his neck and kiss him.

…choose to take a leap of faith.

ᘒ

"I kissed him. In the middle of the fucking street like I was in some ridiculous romantic comedy," I say to

Sophia and Margo as we continue to pack up Sophia's townhouse.

"What did he say?" Margo asks as she holds up her wine glass taking this moment to relax a bit.

"He said he thought it would take longer than a day for him to wear me down."

"So did I." Sophia walks by with several vases balanced in her arm. "Who needs eighteen vases? Why do I have so many of these?"

"Because people have sent you a shit load of flowers over the years and you get rid of nothing," Margo says as she separates the Waterford from the glass. "Back to Cami. What are you going to do about this interesting development?"

"I don't know. I have known him for almost twenty-four hours and I can't help but think that I don't want to not have him in my life. This is crazy. Completely crazy that a man I just met can affect me this way. Ever since…"

"Ever since Joseph. I know it is hard for you. You can't keep closing yourself off to any emotional connection with a guy because of something that was out of your control." Sophia clears her throat from the dust.

"I know, but I should be concentrating on my career right now. I should not be letting a guy who will be leaving in a couple of weeks get into my head."

"You have been worried about your career since the moment you learned to read." Sophia says.

"So what? I have never been one of those girls that spent time dreaming out my ideal wedding. I was too busy practicing my speech for winning a National Book Award. I don't need a man to fill in the gaps. I never have."

"And that is great. But now that you are having feelings for *this* guy, I am afraid that you are going to do anything you can to sabotage this."

"Don't be ridiculous Sophia," Margo adds. "She would have to shop in a mall if she lived in the sticks. You know that is never going to happen."

"True. But answer me this, Cami. Why not?" Sophia stops what she is doing to turn her full attention to me.

"Why not what?" I ask as I stuff crumpled newspaper into a box.

"Why not jump? Give this guy a chance. Forget about Joseph, Patrick and any other hand-ups you have. Just take a leap of faith."

"I don't know," I mumble.

"After spending the day with him, do you want to call him right now?" Sophia asks.

"Yes."

"Then go with it. Don't over think this. Do you think that William and I would be together if I didn't think outside of my dating comfort zone?"

"Hell no. I remember your 'Must Haves' list from back in college. It was scary specific," Margo says.

"Didn't you base that list after Judd Neslon's character in the *Breakfast Club*?" I ask.

"I was going through a John Hughes phase and you know I love a bad boy. But we are not talking about how delusional I was in my early twenties. We are dealing with Cami's bag of crazy."

"You are going to need more liquor if you are going to deal with my shit," I say popping open the third bottle of wine tonight.

"Fill 'er up!" Sophia slides her empty glass toward me.

After what seems like hours of packing and drinking, the three of us switch to more drinking and talking than packing. It isn't until after one o'clock in the morning that we all lie down on whatever piece of furniture isn't covered in bubble wrap or boxes. Staring up at her ceiling, I keep thinking about what Sophia said to me. She is right. I never give into my emotions. In the past, my mind has never let there be more in the positive column than the negative when I am dating. But didn't this last year teach me anything?

"Stop over thinking it and go to sleep." Sophia throws a pillow at my head.

Chapter Sixteen

FOR THE LAST TWO WEEKS, I HAVE SPENT MOST of my time divided up between attempting to write, spending time with Jake, and helping Sophia move out of her townhouse. It is really emotional for her even though she tries to hide it. Making the decision to sell her family home was not an easy one. Yet when she puts her mind to something, watch out. I think that her need to try to start a new chapter of her life is overriding her attachments to the home. Her strength amazes me daily. Not only is she dealing with all the emotions in her head, but she even finds the time to give me all the kicks in the ass that I need when I try to find something wrong with Jake.

Since our coffee and trip to The Strand, things have been moving really quickly with him. Sometimes, I think it is too quick. At night, we have been crashing in my apartment. Even on the days when he is working or dealing with his family, no matter what the time, he is with me curled up watching James Corden or re-runs of the *Daily Show*. It almost feels like a *real* adult relationship. It has been a while since I have had one of those. Luckily for me, his production schedule got pushed back another two weeks, so I don't have to deal with saying goodbye just yet.

But today is something entirely different. Today is *the* day. It is the day that I wake up, get dressed, and walk back into the world of publishing. I have had my outfit picked out for days and approved by all the girls. My thoughts are clearly formed and for the first time in forever, I feel as if I have something that someone else wants. Since the initial email, Katrina and I have gone back and forth about what the editors want from me. It boils down to this. They are interested in having me write a serial where I would be telling a story over a number of weeks. Then if it takes off, I will do another one.

As I step out of the cab in front of the tall glass building, my phone pings with a text. Quickly glancing down to see that Jake sent a photo of himself with a thumbs up that warms my heart. *What a goofball.* I send him back a quick line of emoji smiley faces and kissing faces. Then, put my phone on silent and back in my bag.

When I look up, I notice that across the street is where I saw the sign "Coming Soon… Patty Publishing" when I was out with Sophia that day. Only now it looks as if the publishing house is open. I should have called Patrick. There might have been a job opening there for me, but there was something nagging at me. Why didn't he call me? Sure, I had texts from him a while back, but after the intervention it has been radio silence. I even texted him once to thank him for the manuscript. *Come to think of it…where did I put that? Nope. No distractions. You must focus on the task at hand.*

Composing myself, I smooth out my coat and head through the revolving doors. The security guard gives me my day pass and sends me up to the twentieth floor. When the doors to the elevator open, a young smiley-faced girl in a see-through white turtleneck sweater and skin-tight black skirt that looks like it should be a headband greets me. "You must be Camilla. We are so excited to have you here."

"Thank you. I can't wait to meet everyone."

"Marissa! How difficult is it to put the correct press release in the correct folder?" A woman in head-to-toe Chanel stops dead in her tracks. "And this is?"

"I am Camilla Valentini," I say as I hold my hand out to shake hers hesitantly.

"Good. Good. Now you I can work with." Turning

around the woman heads down the hall and vanishes through a doorway.

"Who was that?" I ask the girl who looks as if she is going to burst into tears.

"That is…is…"

"Here." I hand her a pack of tissues.

"Thank you. That is Mary Smithson. She is the publicist and agent to many of our writers. I believe they called her in to talk to you. Why don't you take a seat, and I will let Katrina know you are here."

"Sounds good. Thanks." I go to sit down on the sofa, but soon realize that it is way too low for me to be able to get back up without showing the staff what color my underwear is. So I opt for standing while I look at the wall of framed awards and past covers.

"Camilla! It is so good to finally meet you." A woman around my age with a pixie haircut and man-tailored suit puts out her hand for me to shake. "Are you ready for this?"

"As ready as I will ever be."

We head down the hallway and into the room that I saw Mary disappear into earlier. Glancing around, I can see that there are three people in the room other than myself and Katrina. *He is here. Why is he here?*

Katrina starts the introductions. "This is Layla Undine Chisisi. She is a senior editor and will be working very closely with you."

"Nice to meet you," Layla says with a hint of an accent that I can't quite place, but judging by her exotic look, I am thinking it might be the Middle East. Maybe Egypt. The way that she outlines her eyes with liner reminds me of depictions of Cleopatra.

"I believe that you met Mary. She handles all of the PR for our writers."

"Yes. This can work. I am glad that you didn't bring me another one of those makeovers again. I love writers, but as a people, you all rarely know how to dress." Mary continues to size me up.

"And this is…"

"Hello, love." Patrick steps out of the shadows of the room and is but inches from me when he says, "I am glad that you could make it."

"Patrick. What are you…" As I start to say it, I remember that LORD Publications was in the running to acquire this magazine. I didn't know that the deal was done, but judging by Patrick's presence, I guess they did.

"Oh good. You know Mr. Lord. He is standing in for the new publisher. Now that the introductions are done, let's get down to business."

For the next hour and a half, I sit talking with Layla, Katrina, and Mary about what they thought would be a good plot for the story and I throw out a few suggestions that I have. Mary touches upon how I will have to start making myself known on social media. Patrick, however, has been silent. He has not said one word the entire time we are hashing everything out.

As if he is reading my mind, Patrick finally speaks up. "This is all very good. Does everyone have what they need? I think I would like to speak with Ms. Valentini alone for a moment."

"Mr. Lord?" Katrina asks as if she were left out of the loop.

"My father is Mr. Lord. Call me Patrick," he states, causing her to blush. "You ladies have done a wonderful job, but I think that Camilla may not be ready for one of our marathon sessions without some caffeine. Why don't you all grab some coffee and take a break?"

When the last one exits the room, he shuts the door. "Before you even—"

"What are you doing here Patrick? I haven't heard from you in months and now you happen to show up at my meeting. Why?"

"Easy there, love. I had nothing to do with getting you in here if that is what you were thinking. I only took advantage of the opportunity to see you when I saw that the meeting was set up. They don't bring in Mary for just anyone, so I am always interested in seeing who the new writing star is. Much to my surprise and delight it is you."

"So this is just a happy accident? Because if you wanted to see me, you could have called." I am visibly flustered by all his Patrick-ness.

"This is just business, but in case you were wondering, I did try to call you. You hung up on me."

"I didn't hang up on you. What the hell are you talking about?"

"One night about two weeks ago. I called you and as soon as I said hello, you hung up."

"No I di… That was you? I was out with the girls at a bar watching rugby. My phone cut out on me. The reception was horrible." I stop for a minute to think if I ever checked my incoming calls. The only thing I remembered from that night was Jake's arms were wrapped around me and staring into his baby blues. Shaking my head, I see that Patrick is just staring at me. "What?"

"You were in a bar watching rugby?"

"Yes. What's your point?"

"Nothing. You never cease to surprise me."

"You don't know everything about me."

"I am beginning to see that. Now, if you don't mind, I would like to show you something." He waggles his eyebrows.

"Patrick, I know what you have to offer and I am currently not interested."

"Though I love that your mind went there, I have something else to show you."

"I wasn't talking about—"

"I know, love. But you can't blame a guy for wanting you to." He smiles.

I am following him into the elevator, when I see that the girl at the front desk perks up. Now I know why she is wearing that outfit. Everyone wants to land a Lord.

Patrick completely ignores her as we enter through the doors. I am surprised to see that he presses the ground level. *He is taking me across the street.*

Escorting me out the doors, we cross the street to the building that is now housing Patty Publishing.

"Entre, madame." Patrick holds open the door as I pass. "Welcome to Patty Publishing."

The lobby is beautiful. There are rich purple velvet couches and walls of book shelves waiting to be filled with new publications. The front desk has a woman in cat-framed glasses sitting reading on a tablet. This is all very Patrick.

"I have been working on the idea of a publishing house separate from the umbrella of LORD Publications for a while. Dear Old Dad thinks it is a horrible idea, so naturally I had to do it."

"Patrick. This is amazing. Congratulations."

"I did this for you. Because of you."

"What?"

"Of course, I wanted to do this to stick it to Pops, but I did this because of you. I found the story you started writing for me all those years ago. You know, the one that I gave back to you the night of the intervention?" He searches my face for recognition.

"Um…yeah." I remember seeing the pages of a manuscript that I lost with red line edits all over it. *Where did I put that envelope?*

"It started me thinking about authors like you that

work tirelessly to get their pieces published. Many of them never do. I want to be a place that recognizes their natural talent and giving them the chance to be published. To have a book in a bookstore and not just on their laptop."

"This is amazing. I am so proud of you." I give him a hug before I pull away.

"You and me, Cami. We can take the publishing industry by storm." He holds my hand and looks into my eyes. "You and me."

"Patrick…" I say looking around at all that he has done.

"You and me, Cami. I was an idiot to let you walk out of my life all those years ago. And now we are here. Together. I know I have pulled back from you, but that isn't because I don't care. I needed to get my shit together. I think we can make this great. We can make us great."

There is such hope in his eyes. I cannot tell if it is for the business or us. For years, I wanted this moment to happen. I wanted him to realize that he made a huge mistake all those years ago and now…

"Jake." I look out the window past the poster boards announcing three books coming soon and see Jake peering back at us. Next thing I know, the door is flying open and Jake is heading right for Patrick.

"You entitled son of a bitch. I am going to—"

"Jake. Stop. Nothing is going on." I move myself directly between the two of them, but closer to Jake than Patrick.

"Love. Who is this?" Patrick says as if he is amused at the thought of this man throwing a punch at him.

"Patrick. This is Jake. We are dating. Jake. This is Patrick. His family owns LORD Publications. We used to work together and his company just bought the magazine I had the meeting at."

"This isn't the address that you said your meeting was at. Why are over here?" As I rest my hands on his chest, Jake begins to calm down, but I still see his fists clenching.

"He just wanted to show me his new publishing company. Nothing is going on." Saying the words makes me wonder. What would have happened if Jake wasn't at the window? Would Patrick have wanted me back? Did I even want him back? Or is this all business?

"Well. Congratulations, man. I am sure that it will be a big success. Cami and I wish you the best. You ready to go?" Jake puts his arm around my shoulder in a 'this is my girl' possessive type of way and I am not sure that I like it.

"Um. Yeah." I wiggle out of his grip and turn to Patrick who is more stunned than anything. "I should get going. Again, congratulations on all of this. I am really proud of you."

Heading out the door, my head is spinning. *What the hell just happened?*

"Why are you here?" This comes out way more defensive than I anticipated.

"Wow. I take time away from the bar and my family to come here to support you. Now, I am the one on trial."

"I am not questioning your motives. I just didn't expect you to be here."

"Obviously. If you knew that I was going to be here you wouldn't have just got caught lovingly staring into that guy's eyes."

"I wasn't—"

"You may not have been, but he was. Do you have feelings for this guy?"

"Patrick is in my past. I said there is nothing going on. Why is it so difficult for you to trust me on this?"

"How can I trust you? You say nothing was happening, but what I saw looked like something was about to happen. If he said he wanted to be with you right now, would you want go back to him?"

"He is a friend. I am not going to cut him out of my life because you don't like him. I have known you for minutes compared to how long I have known Patrick."

"Hey. I have no problem with the guy as long as he knows you are not available. But you haven't answered my question."

"It is complicated."

"So basically you want both of us on reserve in case the other one bails."

"Seriously? You really don't know me at all." I shake my head in frustration.

"What is that supposed to mean?"

"I am deluding myself thinking that we have any type of real connection. Maybe in Hollywood a couple of weeks is the longest relationship ever, but here in the non-celebrity world of regular people…" I take a minute to breathe before I say something that I will not be able to take back. "I like you. I really do, but…"

"But what, Cami? You don't know if we have a future or maybe you are just too scared that our connection is more real than what you and British Ken Doll ever had."

"That is not fair."

"I can't do this now." He runs his fingers through his hair. "I have to work at the bar tonight. I will see you tomorrow."

"Jake. Wait." But he doesn't. He just keeps on walking away. I turn and stare at the glass building where Patrick just turned my life upside-down again. "Shit."

Chapter Seventeen

"WHY DOES EVERY PIVOTAL MOMENT WITH HIM seem like some sort of movie scene? I turn into Meg freakin' Ryan every time we are in the streets having a discussion. Ugh!"

"You are being dramatic. Here." Sophia shoves a red Solo cup filled with wine in my hand.

"Can you let me have this for a moment?"

"Fine. Continue on. Act five. Scene three. Action!"

"Funny. I was happy with Jake. I wanted…I want to be with him."

"What if Jake wasn't there outside the window?" William comes in from the kitchen with a bag of chips and another bottle of wine.

"What?" Sophia and I ask in unison.

"What if you were standing there with Patrick, and Jake wasn't there to storm in?"

"I thought about that. I don't know."

"Maybe that is your answer." William sits with his arm around Sophia. "Maybe this thing with Jake is going too fast for you and you are not comfortable with the lack of control you have falling for someone so quickly. Patrick is an easy scapegoat. You have known him for a while and you know his flaws. It would be the second chance for you and him. Jake is the wildcard that came in with the passion and excitement. He scares you."

"Soph. This one is a keeper."

"I know." She smiles at William which is my cue to get the hell out of here.

"Okay. So, I am going to—"

"No you are not. You are staying here with us. You have already destroyed our date night. The least you can do is pack up some more of my crap."

๑๑

The smell of coffee instantly wakes me up. Sophia is in her kitchen for most likely the last time, preparing breakfast.

"Something smells good," I say, yawning while I stretch out my arms.

"I knew I could get you up with the aroma of coffee. How are you feeling this morning?"

"Okay. I guess. I have no idea what the hell I am going to do with my personal life, but the magazine sent over the contract for me to review. I suppose you can't have it all."

"Please don't hate me for saying this, but I think you just need to concentrate on your career for a while."

"You. The girl who has tried to sign me up for online dating and sent me on countless blind dates want me to just worry about work?"

"I know. But here is the thing. I have this feeling like it is all going to work out. You just need to concentrate on you with no other distractions for a while. I feel it in my gut."

"I think you might be right."

"Hello, ladies." Will walks in and kisses Sophia.

"Ewww. I haven't even had my coffee yet." I make my best kid catching her parents kissing face.

"Shut it or I will send you to your room without pancakes." Sophia waves the spatula in my face.

"That reminds me. Can I check the room I was staying in?"

"Sure. Why?"

"Meeting up with Patrick again has me thinking about the envelope that he gave me when you all were telling me I was a mess."

"Didn't you take that with you?"

"I thought I did, but I can't remember where I put it. The last place I know I had it was in that room."

"Go forth and find your lost item." Sophia says with way more dramatic flair than should be used this early in the morning.

Heading down the hallway, I can't help but remember all the years spent in this house. Some were good and others were more difficult. Yet we always managed to make it through. Maybe that is the lesson to everything. You just have to keep moving forward no matter what shit happens along the way.

I enter the room that I spent countless hours in. It is so different with the curtains missing and only a few pieces of furniture remaining. Long gone are any touches of personality. Now. *Where could that envelope be?*

The first places I look are in the drawers of the dresser and the night table. Nothing. Then I check the closet, but I am pretty sure that if something was in there, Will or Sophia would have found it. Next, I lay on my stomach to look under the bed. *Jackpot!* There it is. I manage to wiggle my shoulder and arm under the box frame and grab the package.

Feeling better, I get up and walk down to the kitchen where Sophia is putting a gigantic stack of pancakes on a plate.

"Did you find it?"

"Yeah. It was under the bed."

"So what now? Are you going to do something with it?"

"I think so." I sit at the table. "I hope so."

…something you thought was lost will come back to you. Pay attention to this. There are voices other than your own that you need to listen to. Find out their story.

It has been twenty-four hours since I last heard from Jake. Since we have met, this is the longest we have gone without talking. I want to text him, but I don't know what to say. I could say I am sorry, though I don't think I did anything wrong. Shouldn't he be texting me?

Not knowing what else to do, I decide to go to his family's bar under the guise of bringing back his sister's shoes. For some reason they have been sitting in my closet this whole time, so what could possibly be a better excuse?

Pushing open the door, my eyes need to adjust from the brightness outside to the barroom glow. And there he is. Jake is standing behind the bar, drying off some glasses when he sees me.

"Hi. I brought back your sister's shoes." I hold up the bag and gesture for him to take it.

"Thanks. I am sure that she will be happy to have them back. Can I get you something?"

"It is ten in the morning."

He shrugs and pours two glasses with bourbon. When he comes from around the bar he sits at one of the tables and slides a drink over to me.

"Listen, I just wan—"

"Cami." Jake looks at me and I don't want to know what he is about to say.

"Yeah?" I look down into the brown liquid and ice as I swirl the glass around.

"I was an idiot. I had no right to act like a teenage girl going off on you like that. I just…" He puts his hand on the bar. "I just thought that we were going somewhere and seeing you with that guy snapped me into reality. We have known each other for less than a month. I don't know what I was expecting."

"Nothing happened with Patrick and I."

"And I believe you. I really do. It is just that I don't know where this is going to go."

"Because you are leaving?"

"There is that. It is also because this movie could change everything. It could be a complete bust, but there is something that is telling me, my life will not be my own. I may not know you as well as some other people in your life, but I know that you like your privacy. I don't know how you would handle the attention."

"I never really thought about that."

"Neither one of us did. We got caught up in the romance of it all. We fast forwarded to the relationship part without dealing with any of the real issues."

"The love bubble."

"The what?"

"I used to make fun of Sophia because the minute she would meet a new guy, he instantly became the one. She is known for her whirlwind affairs where she resides in her love bubble."

"I guess that makes sense. I just really like you. And this," he said as he moves his hand back and forth. "I have never felt this type of instant connection before."

"For what it is worth, I feel it too. Taking a leap of faith with you is something that I don't do. In fact, it is the opposite of what I normally do."

"Yeah," he says as he runs his hands through his hair.

"So, where do we go from here?" Part of me not does not want to know the answer to that question. If only we could live in the bubble just a little longer.

"I don't know. I do know that it isn't fair for me to expect you will not date other people when I am filming. No matter how much that pisses me off."

"The idea of you with another woman doesn't exactly make me do the running man."

"I guess we could be friends."

"I don't know if I can do that."

"So what do you want to do?"

"Maybe we can try and see if we can make it work?"

"Are you sure that you want to try a long-distance relationship with someone you have only been dating a month?"

"When you put it like that it doesn't sound too promising. But why not?"

"Why not?" He stands up and goes back to the bar. "Because I can't do that to you. For as much as this is killing me, I need to let you go."

Feeling the tears well up in my eyes, I stand up and lean over the bar to give him a kiss on the cheek. "Bye, Jake."

At the door, I sneak one last look at Jacob O'Leary, the bartender before I completely loose it. This is the guy that helped me realize that I have to open my heart more, even if I get hurt. The guy that I fell in love with at first sight.

I am so going to need two gallons of ice cream and a *Fast and Furious* marathon to get over this one. Nothing like mint chocolate chip, Vin Diesel, and car chases to get your mind off a guy.

Chapter Eighteen

THE NEXT FEW MONTHS FLY BY AS I DIVE INTO MY work for the magazine. Layla is truly amazing to work with. She has a blunt, sometimes harsh, but always honest evaluation of my work that seems to be a good fit for me. Checking my email this morning, there is nothing for me to deal with besides a few comments from my followers and to write the conclusion to the story. I have been putting this off for a week because I just cannot figure out the ending. I have two options and neither one seems like a good fit. No matter how many times I sit down to write it, my mind goes to Patrick and Jake.

It has been radio silent on the guy front. Neither Patrick nor Jake have reached out. Not that I expected to hear from Jake. He made it clear that we were over. Though I have been slightly cyberstalking them both since Mary has gotten me hooked on Instagram and Twitter. The few photos that I have seen posted of Jake working out and bulking up for his part as America's next sexy superhero have him looking even better than I remember. Patrick's accounts aren't as visually stimulating. However, within the last week he has posted photos of late nights at clubs on Instagram. I have not gone as far as to follow either of them, but part of me wonders what would happen if I did. Just as I hover over the follow button for the verified account of Jacob O'Leary, I pull my hands away and close my laptop. *You are not doing this.*

Standing up, I decide to clean my apartment. Whenever I am blocked or upset, this is what I do. You would think that my place would be spotless with the neurosis, but it is surprisingly unkempt lately.

After a complete apartment clean-up, I sit back down at my desk. I am not getting the ending done to this story today, but maybe I can finally make some time for that manuscript that has been taunting me. I grab the black and white folder from my desk organizer and sitting cross-legged on my floor start to read the pages that I worked on so long ago.

An hour later, I am staring at the last sentence of the stack of papers in complete shock. This was the book I was working on just before the fire. I had pulled it out to see if there was something I could salvage, but I thought it went up in flames with all the others. When I first started the book, I was working for Theo, but I didn't think I gave a copy to Patrick. Sure, during the time we were seeing each other, he used to be in the habit of reading my work whether I wanted him to or not. He never said anything about the work. All he did was read them and return pages back to where he found them. Sometimes, he would make edits like he did with this one, but that was rare.

The pages in front of me are much more vivid than I remember. Though, this is more of a plot outline and character study than a cohesive narrative. I see the story that needs to be told. Quickly, I gather up the papers with the notes that I started to make in the margins around page three and open up my laptop. The twitter feed with Jake's face comes to life and I stare at it for just a moment longer. I would like to say that I don't still love him. I would like to be completely over the whole thing, but I am not. I miss him. I miss his smile and the way he used to make me laugh. I miss his arms around me at night. With one more glance, I close out my browser to open a blank document.

It seems that without fail, every time I start typing, my phone rings. Now is no different. I pick up the phone, but the number doesn't look familiar. Normally I would let it go to voicemail, but I decide to pick it up anyway. I am feeling good and if a telemarketer wants to get into it, today is definitely the day.

"Hello?"

Nothing.

"Hello?"

Nothing. But this time I can swear I hear something in the background.

"Anyone?" My new writing buzz is starting to wear off as I get more and more pissed.

Nothing.

"Listen, pervert, if you are trying to get your jollies off by calling random women and not saying anything than screw you. Anything? Do you have anything to say for yourself?"

Click.

"Well, fuck you too then." I slam down my phone and take my frustrations out on my computer keys.

When I emerge from my writing haze, I realize that it is now dark outside and I am starving. I have retyped the pages from the yellow envelope along with some additions to help kick start the beginning of the book, so I have earned some much needed carbs. I head to my fridge and take out the frozen lasagna I make for days like this. I pre-heat the oven and wait for the temperature to reach 400. It is killing me how long this oven takes to get to a decent temperature. I decide to take my mind off of it and pour a glass of wine for myself. Roaming around my apartment, my eyes keep going back to the manuscript open on my laptop. The characters are speaking to me. Juliet is speaking to me. I can see the way she walks and how she interacts with people. I can see how she treats Declan's family. Everything is so clear to me.

Beep. Beep. Beep.

The oven breaks my train of thought, but only for as long as it takes to pop in the tray of deliciousness and to set the timer. I am back at my computer typing away, taking breaks only to have a sip of wine here and there. *Hemingway always said write drunk, edit sober.*

Chapter Nineteen

BANG. BANG. BANG.

"Camilla Valentini, you open this door right now." Sophia's voice breaks my train of thought.

"Soph?" I stand up and stretch as I head to open the door.

"You are alive." Jenny makes an over dramatic gesture as she pushes her way inside. "But you smell like you are not."

"When was the last time you left this place?" Paula looks around as if searching for the hidden clue to me being MIA for the past three weeks.

"I think that the better question is when was the last time you bathed?" Margo pinches her nose with her fingers.

"Very funny. You all are hilarious."

"No seriously. You need to take a shower before we continue this conversation. What exactly have you been doing up here?"

Lifting my arm to smell myself, I start to count back the last day I showered. It was only three days ago. No, four. No, it has definitely been three days. "Okay. Give me five minutes."

"Take ten. You will thank us," Margo says as she opens the cabinets in my kitchen, pulling out some crackers.

As I emerge smelling more human than orc. "I see that you all have helped yourself to my food."

"And drinks. You know we love our booze after five." Jenny holds up her glass.

"You like your booze before five too." Paula gives her a side glance.

"So. Why have you gone off the grid?" Sophia cuts to the chase. "We haven't seen you in, what, three weeks? You barely answer your texts. We are—"

"Stop." I hold up my hand. "Look around. I am not going off the rails or in some sort of un-Cami like tailspin."

"Then why?" Sophia asks.

"Because of this." I hand her a print-out of the almost completed manuscript.

"*Yours, Mine, and the Truth.*"

"What is that?" Bobby asks as all five of them huddle around the stack of papers in Sophia's hands.

"It is my book. I have one more pass to do, but it is my book."

"Holy shit, Cam! This is amazing. Can I read it?"

"No. I am the only other writer here. I get first crack at it." Bobby tries to grab the pages.

"Actually. None of you will be reading it." I pry the book from Sophia. "Yet."

"But, Cami…" Jenny whines.

"There is someone who has to read it first."

"And who would that someone be?" Sophia's eyebrow raises.

❧

"Miss. You cannot just go in there. Miss." A perky twenty-something is chasing me down the hallway as I make a right into Patrick's office. "I am so sorry, Mr. Lord. She just—"

"It's alright." He waves her away without even giving a glance up.

"Here." I plop down three hundred and fifty-two pages in a brown file-folder on his desk.

"What is this?"

"This is what was in the yellow envelope you gave me."

"Sit." He gestures to the chair across from him. "I remember it being a lot lighter than this."

"It was."

"And…"

"And now it is more than that. I have spent the last three weeks of my life living and breathing these characters. I know them better than I know my own family."

"Really?"

"Are you just going to use one word responses or can we have a conversation here?"

"Camilla." Patrick leans forward on his desk. "This is why I am here."

"What?"

"This." He holds up the book and waves it in the air. "This is why I created this company. This is the reason why I have stepped away from my father's company and am doing this all on my own. Your words. Your characters. They are what sparked my passion for doing more than reviewing layouts and studying analytics."

"I…this is…thank you. You believing in me…"

He walks around his desk and looks directly into my eyes. "You don't have to say anything else. But I do need to say this. So just let me get it out."

"Okay."

"When I was with you some seven odd years ago, you changed me. I didn't realize it until I lost you, but you set in motion something that I never thought would happen. I started to grow up. You said that you had to leave

LORD because my father and Claudia were treating you differently."

"Yes. I assumed that they thought I wasn't good enough for you."

"Ha! That's rich. They thought you were out of my league. Dear Old Dad even sat down with me after you left and told me that if I couldn't get my shit together that I should let you go. Claudia told me that if I didn't see who you were and what you were capable of doing, I didn't deserve you."

"I…uh…"

"They were right. Or at least I thought they were."

"That is why you never called me again?"

"Then when I bumped into you at that restaurant I thought it was fate telling me that I had another chance. I knew that I might not be able to be with you, but I thought that if I could show you who you really are, then maybe there would be a place for me in your life."

Holy shit. Where was all this coming from?

"And now. Now you brought me your book. This is who you are. You were never supposed to be an assistant or a copy editor. You have always been an author."

"It just took me a while to get there." I smile, looking at the man I wanted for so many years. He is saying everything that I wanted him to say. And now, with no one barging in, I know what would have happened those few months ago.

"What?" He looks at me with his head tilted.

"If you would have said this to me seven years ago or even one year ago, I think that I might have kissed you."

"And now?"

"I just want to hug you." I get up from where I am sitting and wrap my arms around him. "You know me better than a lot of people and I cannot think of anyone better to be the first one to read my book."

"Sophia hasn't even read it?" He displays an over exaggerated shocked pose.

"Nope. That honor goes to you, Patty."

"Oh, you know I love it when you call me that."

"I should get going. I have a holiday party at my aunt's place."

"Sounds like a blast."

"Would you like to come?"

"Me?"

"Yeah. I think it might be fun. The girls will be there. Not to mention, my aunt cooks enough food for twenty extra guests."

"Are you sure? I don't want anyone getting the wrong idea."

"Oh sure you do. You would like nothing better, but I am inviting you anyway."

"So what is this now?" Patrick asks as we enter the elevator.

"What is what?"

"Us."

"We are friends."

"With benefits?"

"Nice try. Just friends."

Entering my family's holiday party is like entering a war zone. And walking in with Patrick is like stepping on a landmine. All eyes are on us from the minute we walk in the door. I quickly escort us over to Sophia and William who are with my Aunt JoJo.

"Cami." Sophia reaches to give me a hug and then whispers in my ear, "Is there something that you want to tell me?"

"Aunt JoJo, I believe that you know Patrick."

"Nice to see you again," my aunt says.

"Patrick, this is William. Sophia's boyfriend."

"Nice to meet you." Patrick shakes his hand. "Any idea where the drinks are? I have a feeling we are going to need something soon."

"I'll show you." Will takes his cue from Sophia's pointed glare.

"What are you doing?" Sophia turns to me.

"I delivered the book to Patrick before I came. Then I invited him."

"So is this a date?" Aunt JoJo asks while picking at the selections from the antipasto.

"No."

"No?" Sophia asks.

"No. This is not a date. We are just friends. I want it that way."

"So there is nothing going on with you two? You are just two friends that use to sleep together seven years ago." Margo comes up from behind them with Bobby trailing her.

"I was in Patrick's office and I kept thinking back to what he said in the lobby of his building. He was telling me everything I wanted to hear, but when I handed him the manuscript today, I just felt that the emotions I was so unsure about weren't there anymore. He was being the guy that I wanted him to be. But…"

"But…" Bobby leans in.

"Nothing. There was no spark or butterflies. There was just what I feel when I am around you weirdos."

"So what now?" Bobby asks.

"Now. We eat!" I say as I make my way to the tables with all the food.

"And drink." Patrick comes up behind us and hands me a glass of wine.

"Winos unite!" Jenny holds up her glass with pride.

And for a moment, I can swear that I see Patrick checking her out. *I didn't see that one coming.* I introduce Jenny to Patrick and slip away as I let the two of them continue to talk without me.

When I get home, I kick my heels off into my closet, get out of my dress, and put on my comfiest pjs. I am completely stuffed and a little tipsy. Who am I kidding? I am drunk. Drunk enough that it seems like a good idea to see what Jake is doing on Instagram. Turning on my tablet, I sign into the app and type in his handle.

My heart sinks. There in front of me is Jake with his co-star in the Bahamas. There are photos of them lying poolside, on the beach, and with friends at dinner. The latest photo updated twenty minutes ago has her kissing his cheek while she takes the photo. I throw the tablet on the table and turn on the TV. I am thinking a few episodes of *Buffy* will get me back into the right headspace.

If I was from Paris, I would say: Oh-la-la-la-la-la-la-la, Oh-la-la-la-la-la-la, Oh-la-la-la-la-la-la, Oh-la-la-la-la-la-la...
The ring of my phone wakes me up at five o'clock. I have to figure out how to change that. I love Grace Potter And The Nocturnals just as much as the next person, but not when I am hung over, dry mouthed, and stuck in a weird position on my couch.

"Hello?"

"Love. Did I wake you?"

"Uh…no…I'm up. What's the matter?"

"Nothing is the matter. Everything is perfect. I have read about half of your book."

"Really? And…"

"And you need to send the manuscript to Layla to start editing. I will have a contract to you tomorrow. You did it, Cami. Now go back to sleep. Talk to you later."

Click.

What just happened?

Suddenly, I am wide awake when it hits me. I am going to be published. I jump up from my couch and start dancing around the room.

Picking up my phone again, I do a conference call with Margo, Bobby, Sophia, Paula, Jenny, my parents, and Aunt JoJo. On hearing the chorus of hellos, I scream. "I am going to be a real author! I did it!" Then I drop the phone and dance around some more.

Chapter Twenty

Two years later.

"I CANNOT BELIEVE THAT IT HAS BEEN TWO YEARS since you published *Yours, Mine, and the Truth*," Sophia says as we walk into the restaurant.

"I can't believe that you are living in the suburbs. The city weeps."

"You are such a drama queen. It is only forty-five minutes away."

"It is New Jersey," Margo says as she greets us.

"Cami!" Jenny pulls away from Patrick and runs over.

"Tonight is going to be amazing. Did you know that they had to turn people away?"

Tonight is the anniversary party for *Yours, Mine, and the Truth*. The Patty Publishing is re-releasing the book with a new cover, an interview with me, and a never before published short story at the end. I am still amazed every time someone tells me they loved the book or that they would love to see it made into a movie. My die-hard fans are the best though. Most are New Yorkers and will yell my name across the street like we have known each other for years.

Turning into the restaurant, the whole gang is there. Sophia, Margo, and Jenny are by my side. Layla is talking with Bobby. Patrick is standing with someone at the bar. Paula is talking with her mom, Aideen. My parents are smiling and laughing as they talk to my Aunt JoJo. I never thought this day would come.

Three years ago, I was obsessed with all the things that I didn't have and that were going wrong in my life. Then I realized that I cannot control everything. This moment freed me. It allowed me to move forward from my past, take a leap of faith, and choose to make my own path. I still have control issues, just ask my editors, but I take more pleasures in the not knowing or the missteps that I have made.

"You ready for this?" Patrick comes up to me, breaking my moment of reflection.

"I think so. There are a lot of people here."

"A lot of people want to meet you. You keep burrowing yourself up in your writer's cave. People are starting to think you are a hermit or have agoraphobia."

"Just tell them that I like my *me* time and I write best alone while drinking vats of coffee."

"I like it. I think we should add it to your bio."

"Sounds like a plan. Now let's get this party started."

Patrick takes my enthusiasm as an all systems go and runs up on the makeshift stage. "Ladies and gentlemen. Thank you all for coming here tonight. It is a special book that brings critics and readers together with their praise. From the moment I read the beginning of this book almost nine years ago, I knew it would be something special. And now, because you all aren't here to see this gorgeous face"—the crowd laughs—"I would like to introduce you to the lady of the hour. Miss Camilla Valentini."

You did it. You really did it.

Tonight is one of those nights that is both exciting, fun, and really, really tiring. Exiting the town car, I just want to get upstairs, get comfy, and curl up with a good book. For some reason, when I get home for these events, my desire to jump into someone else's world is such a pull. Now is the perfect time to dive into one of the books in my ever-growing stack on my nightstand. I wonder who it will be? It could be the latest Lestat novel by Anne Rice or one of the Alpha One Security romances by Jasinda Wilder or maybe Marissa Myer's newest book, *Heartless*. Of course, there is always the neatly stacked pile of advanced reading copies in a basket on the floor next to my couch. The excitement of a new book to read completely distracts me. Before I know it, I am tripping over a man sitting on the stoop to my building.

"Seriously? What the hell?" I look down and underneath the Yankees baseball cap, I see blue eyes staring back at me. Those God damn blue eyes.

"Hey, Cami."

"Jake? What are you doing here? Shouldn't you be on some set or yachting with the fabulous people?"

"Yeah. You would think, but I got injured on set and they gave me a couple weeks off. As for the yachting, that is not really my thing."

"Oh, I forgot. You are more of a romping around the beach with a size-two model type of guy these days."

"That is not fair."

"I'm sorry. It is just that it has been what two years and I have heard nothing from you. It took me a while to move on from what we had. As brief as it was, I loved you. I jumped and fell flat on my ass."

"You loved me?"

"Jake. I have had a really great night, and right now, I just can't do this." I push past him and start to open the door.

"I just missed you. That is all. I missed you," he mumbles as he starts to walk away.

"Are you drunk?" I ask.

"No. Are you?"

"A little bit." I hold my pointer finger and thumb hovering over one and other.

"I missed you." He walks back up the steps and stands inches away from my body.

"It has been over two years, Jake. Why now?"

"Why not?"

"Because…Because…Well, I don't actually have a reason this very moment, but I am sure that I can come up with something."

"Didn't you miss me?"

"I missed you when you left. I missed you for the months after, but if we are being honest, I didn't miss you until I saw you standing here right now."

"What should we do about this?" He gestures between the two of us.

"I don't know." I just had one of the most amazing nights in my professional career. I couldn't have the luck to have my personal life start to look up too. "I think you should go."

"Are you sure?"

"Yes. You should go. I need to clear my head and having you staring at me with those eyes and looking like you do is not going to help me do that."

As he leans close to me, the stubble from his face

tickles mine. "Goodnight, Cami. Sweet dreams." With a soft kiss to my cheek he turns around and walks down the street.

Do not chase him. Don't you dare chase him down the street.

Luckily for me, my resolve to not make this into one of those made-for-TV movies and my aching feet keep me firmly planted on my stoop. I wait there until I can no longer see him. Walking into my building, all I keep thinking is… *Jacob O'Leary is back in New York. I am screwed.*

◌

Surprisingly, I wake up the next morning with a lot more energy than I anticipated. After my encounter with my past, I would have thought that I would want to curl up on my couch watching *Sixteen Candles* with a bowl of popcorn mixed with peanut M&Ms. I have already checked my email and started to open my newest manuscript when I notice a text message from a number that I don't recognize.

It reads: Meet me in Bryant Park at noon. - Jake

I must re-read the text six times before I start to freak out. What does he want? To talk? To tell me…what? Is choosing Bryant Park because of our first date or because he is just near there? *Shit! Shit! Shit!*

The only way I can figure out what to do is make a proper list of pros and cons. Sitting with a pad and pen, I start to outline why I should meet him and why I shouldn't. Topping the cons list are the fact that he ended it with me, he broke my heart, and the celebrity factor. Not to mention his damn Instagram account with kissy faces of co-stars all over it. I am not particularly proud of this fact, but I still look at Jake's account. He recently just posted another one of his fabulous island trips with one of his female co-stars. While I sit alone in my apartment looking like a crazed mountain woman in front of my computer. *Not bitter. Not bitter at all.*

The pros tend to be a bit more superficial. He looks good. I mean really good. Then there are those piercing blue eyes and the simple fact that he was waiting on my stoop to talk to me. He could have tried to call or text me, but Jake sat out there for I don't know how long to see me. When I finish, there are just as many items in both columns, but at the bottom, between both columns, I have one phrase. *He missed me.* I circle it twice before I get up to get ready to meet him at the park.

Meeting in the park in the fall is nice. Meeting in the part in the winter is crazy. Bundled up in my typical try-not-to-freeze-your-ass-off attire, I walk into Bryant Park toward the carousel. For noon on a weekend, the place is pretty quiet.

"Hey," Jake says from behind me.

Turning around, it is hard to see his expression from under the scarf that is wrapped around his face. "Hey."

"So I thought that—"

"Before you finish that. Do you think we can go somewhere with heat?"

"If you let me finish, I was going to say that I made reservations at the restaurant around the corner. A friend of mine owns it and I have been dying to try the food."

"Perfect. I am going to freeze my tits off if we stay out here any longer."

"Now that would be a travesty. Shall we run there?"

"A brisk walk will be fine."

Entering the restaurant is like waking up in the most comfortable bed ever. It is so cozy and warm with the aroma of cinnamon filling my nose.

"This place looks amazing."

"I know, right? She put a lot of work into it and here she is." Jake opens his arms to hug the woman in a chef's coat. "Mariana. It is so good to see you."

"Come in. I have a great table for the two of you." She escorts us in. "I have to thank you, by the way. Joselyn had so much fun on that trip you two took to the islands. I wish I could have made it, but I was hiring staff."

Jake turns to me. "Mariana is Joselyn's girlfriend."

"Wife." Mariana holds up her hand.

"Wife. I forgot you two got hitched last week."

"Joselyn. As in your co-star Joselyn?" A week ago, I wanted to make a voodoo doll of that woman because she was all over his Instagram account. *Oops.*

"Yup." Jake is just looking at me, watching the wheels in my head turn.

"Well, congratulations are in order then." I plaster on my largest smile and sit in the seat that Jake just pulled out for me.

"I will let the two of you look at the menu and a waiter will be over in a minute."

Quickly, pick up the menu and start reading it. "Everything looks really good. Do you know what you want?"

"I am thinking about the Moroccan chicken and a confession."

"A confession?"

"You had no idea that Joselyn is a lesbian."

"No. I didn't."

"And you saw the photos I posted?" He is looking over the top of his menu and though I can't see his mouth, I know he is smirking.

"I know that this may shock you, but not everyone follows your Instagram account."

"I never said I posted to Instagram."

Damn it.

"Don't worry about it. I suppose congratulations is in order." He smiles. "The re-release party looked really fun."

"It was. I hate doing speeches, so Patrick did most of the talking. But wait...you know about the re-release?" I don't know why I am surprised, but I guess I always figured he just cut me out of his life.

"I follow your accounts too. I have been checking in

from time to time to see what you are doing. It is just my way of making sure you are okay. I even have a first edition copy of *Yours, Mine, and the Truth* on my shelf."

"That couldn't have been too hard to get. It is only two years old."

"I am thinking more long term. Imagine what it will be worth ten or twenty years down the line."

"Probably less than what you paid for it."

"Don't do that. I am sure that there are great things yet to come from you."

"Well, I have a new manuscript due to the publisher in a week, so hopefully you are right. It is completely different from my other three books."

The waiter finally makes his way over to us. "I am Gary and I will be your server today. Can I start you off with an appetizer and something to drink?"

"Yes. We will have two glasses of your best Cabernet and an order of the calamari."

"Very good, sir. I will be right back with your drinks."

"Apparently, in the last two years, I have completely lost the ability to order for myself." I mockingly turn my attention back to Jake.

"I did that, didn't I? I am so used to ordering that I completely forgot to ask. Do you want something else? I'll get him back."

"No. No. It's okay. I am sure that the wine will be fine and I eat pretty much anything, as you may remember."

The tense look on his face starts to fade and then

he said the three words he kept repeating last night. "I missed you."

"So you keep saying."

As soon as the waiter brings the wine over Jake takes a sip. "When I left, I wanted to keep in touch with you. I really did."

"Then why didn't you?" It appears that we are jumping right into this, so I follow his lead and start drinking my wine.

"I tried. A few months after I left, I got a little drunk and called you from my new phone number. When you picked up, I just didn't have the balls to say something. I think you called me a pervert which made me feel like a complete stalker."

"Oh God. I am sorry about that. I hate those no-response phone calls. I tend to get a little pissy with them. But that doesn't explain why you didn't try to text me or something when you were sober."

"Because I couldn't. If I started to talk to you again, I knew that I wouldn't be able to keep away."

"And that is a bad thing."

"It is when I wanted to protect you."

"And now? Things have changed?"

"Before I started filming, I had a feeling of what could happen. But when I was in it on a day-to-day basis, you have no idea. Things blew up so quickly. Suddenly my family and my life were under scrutiny. People were following me everywhere."

"Isn't that sort of what happens when you are a celebrity?"

"Yeah, but I didn't think it was going to be like that. Even now, I have to hide where I am going. Did you know that five people know I am in New York? The rest think that I am off on some European adventure with whatever model they have linked me with this week."

"Wow." I am unable to formulate anything other than that.

"I am getting off track here. I didn't call you because I didn't want my life to change yours."

"Thank you?"

"Then as the months and years kept going by I started to feel more and more alone. I am surrounded by tons of people, but none of them really care about me. My parents, sister, and *real* friends are here in the City and I am…well…it depends on the week. I have thrown myself into my work completely. Then I was walking past a bookstore in San Diego the week I was at Comic-Con. I saw your book sitting in the window with a poster that said you would be there for a signing and interview."

"I remember that. It was so much fun because all the girls were able to take time off of work and come with me. Were you there?"

"Yes. I sat in the back and watched you talk to readers while signing their books. You looked so happy. I wanted to go up and say hello, but I saw you with a guy. You were hugging him and introducing him to everyone. I didn't want to get in between you too."

"I was? Oh…" I suddenly remember. "I was. The guy you are talking about is Paula's brother. I hadn't seen him since he was a teenager."

"So you weren't dating him?"

"No. I wasn't dating him. I really haven't had too much time for dating. But we are not talking about me. Let's just cut through all the bullshit and stories. What is it that you want?"

"I want you."

"You want me to what?"

"No. I just want you. I want to get back to where we were in those two weeks when we first met."

"We can't go back, Jake. Too much time has passed."

"I knew that there was a chance you would say this. I didn't want to believe it, but I knew that I could have blown it."

"We can't go back."

"You already said that."

"Will you let me finish a thought? Geeze! I don't remember you being so annoying." I take a moment to sip the last drop of my wine which appears to have magically disappeared from the glass. "We can't go back, but we can move forward."

"Forward."

"Yes. But this time, we are going to take it slow."

"I can do slow." He waggles his eyebrows.

"Oh dear lord. What is it with the men in my life?" I raise my hand to get the waiter to come back to the table and point to my empty glass. "I am going to need more of this."

"So you were saying we need to take it slow."

"Yes. Borderline glacial. If we are going to try to have any type of relationship, I want to make sure that we don't fuck it up again."

After finishing our lunch, we both decide to take a walk back to my apartment instead of a cab. Suddenly all the wine and good food is making the frigid temperatures a little more bearable. When we reach my stoop, I take a minute to think about how we got here.

A series of horrible events that left me broken, but with help, I was able to get myself out of it. I was able to understand that those events, no matter how many times I want to mentally beat myself up for them, led me to becoming the person I am supposed to be. It can be cliché to say that through adversity your strength and resolve are tested, but that doesn't make it any less true.

The person who I was four years ago was who I wanted people to see. I thought that by orchestrating every part of my life, according to a plan I had, would show everyone who I really was. The person that I am today is a product of falling and getting back up. I found out who I am by losing the control I always wanted to have. This lead me to taking one of the greatest risks in my life. I created something for the world to judge when I gave Patrick that manuscript. It was a gamble, but I did it anyway. I gave my heart to someone without question and for that time we were together, I knew what it was like to be loved. Now, he is standing in front of me looking for me to do it all over again.

"What are you thinking?"

"I could have never planned this," I say. I lean in to kiss him while trying not to let the tears fall from my eyes.

"No you couldn't," Jake says as he wipes away the single tear on my cheek with his thumb.

"I missed you."

Epilogue

Five Years After It Hit The Fan

"THAT WAS A GREAT INTERVIEW, CAMILLA." AIDEEN starts to take off her mic.

"Was it too much? I feel like I might have said a lot of things that I shouldn't have."

"You shared what you needed to. Think of it as an on-camera therapy session."

"I do feel different. I think I might have lost a few pounds from the heat of the lights too."

"You did wonderful!" Mary sweeps onto the set,

already typing something on her phone. "Now how do you feel about making an appearance on *Watch What Happens Live*?"

"That's the one with the liquor and Andy Cohen, right?"

"It is. They had a cancelation for tonight, but before you say no—"

"I will do it." I don't hesitate.

"Cami. Let me just explain how good this will be… Wait. You will do it?"

"Yes. I will do it. I could use a drink anyway. Besides, I just told the whole world everything about my life. How difficult can a few games and some viewer questions be?"

"I am going to call them now. You have time to go home and change. Wear something a little more sexy and fun. Call Margo or Sophia if you need help." With that she is a blur in the dark heading off set.

Once I am finally away from the cameras and out on the street, I take a deep breath of the crisp fall air until a large truck comes barreling down blowing puffs of black smoke causing me to cover up my face with my hand.

If I was from Paris, I would say: Oh-la-la-la-la-la-la, Oh-la-la-la-la-la-la, Oh-la-la-la-la-la-la, Oh-la-la-la-la-la-la…

Five years and I still haven't changed that damn ring tone. "Hello?"

"Hey, hon! How did it go?" Sophia asked.

"Good."

"A good like you were composed and said what you

planned to say or good like we should warn our friends and families of the shit storm that is coming our way."

"I sort of let it all out. It was really cathartic. I don't think I have ever sat down and talked about the past five years before."

"It wasn't for lack of people trying. I guess this was just the time for it."

"Yeah. I just hope that I didn't share too much."

"Don't you have a final edit?"

"This is Aideen we are talking about."

"Oh yeah. She will never let you see it until it airs. What do you think Jake is going to say about it?"

"You can ask him when we drive out to the boonies tomorrow for your County Fair thing."

"He is coming? I wasn't sure if he would make it. Are you bringing the dog too? You know Antonia loves that pup."

"Yessiree!" I say in my best country bumpkin accent.

"Well, y'all better get here early because the cow need-a milkn'," She says in a mocking tone.

"Seriously, Soph. What time do you need us there?"

"Whenever you get here will be fine. Will is going to take Antonia to the morning activities, so I have some down time. She loves running around the pumpkin patch that they have set up."

I love seeing this side of Sophia. In the years since leaving New York, she has become a wife and now a mother. My darling little goddaughter, who is going to be three, is just like her mother. *God help us all.* I always thought that motherhood would tone Sophia down, but she is still the tell-it-like-it-is girl with the razor-sharp tongue I have known since our days back in grammar school. Now she just balances that with Disney Kids and baking cookies.

"Sounds good. Do you need me to bring anything?"

"Unless you can bring me back my sanity, I think I am good."

"The artwork not going the way you want?"

"I have been trying to balance everything, but have been a little distracted. Last night, I almost stirred the soup with my paintbrush."

"Maybe you need a vacation?"

"How about an hour with my best friend and some hot apple cider?"

"I will bring the flask."

"Do you know how much I love you right now? Antonia get out of the stove," Sophia yells away from the phone. "I have to go, but I will see you tomorrow. Antonia! If you don't…"

Click.

I have to say that for the sticks, the town Sophia lives in is really nice. There are coffee shops, a bookstore, clothing boutiques, and at the very end of the town square, Haut Monde Gallery. Paula and Jenny decided to have Sophia run the space to showcase local artists as well as her work.

"This is really nice," Jake says as we walk down the street with Mischief, our shepherd-mastiff mix, pulling every which way, trying to sniff everything in her path.

"Aunt Cami! Mischeeeef!" A little girl screams from the top of the hay stack before Will manages to pull her off. The little feet come charging toward me as we go into the parking lot that they turned into the main area of the fair.

"Hey, munchkin." I scoop her up and twirl her around. "Wow. You are getting big."

"And heavy." William makes his way over to us.

"I am perfect sized. That is what Mummy tells me."

"You are." Sophia comes up behind us as Antonia wiggles out of my arms to go give the dog a hug. The giggles are infectious as the two greet each other.

"This is really cool, Soph," I say with the utmost sincerity that I can tell she is doubting. "I am being honest here. I didn't think they would have so many things. Is that a jewelry stand over there?"

"Oh crap. I hope they take credit cards," Jake says jokingly. I send my death stare at him which immediately causes his arms to fly up in surrender.

"We have a lot of artisans here. I have been pushing the town to send out feelers to them and it looks like they did. I have a number of pieces from the same artists in the gallery."

"Look over there. Is that a fortuneteller?" Jake asks.

"Why yes it is," Sophia says while giving me the side eye.

"What is that look for?" William asks.

"Nothing. Your wife just believes that she is funny. She is not."

"Come on. Let's take a walk about." Jake takes my hand and leads me into the rows of tables.

"A walk about? Are we going all Jane Austen today?"

"You know I like to get into the mindset of my characters before I get on set."

In a month, Jake will be staring in a remake of one of my favorite Jane Austen novels, *Pride and Prejudice*. He was hesitant about taking the part, but after we both read the script and found out that Joselyn is going to be playing opposite him, he decided to sign on. Personally, I can't wait to see him in the full period outfit.

"So does this mean that I will be sleeping with Mr. Darcy tonight?"

"If you play your cards right."

Spending the day at the fair is the most fun that I have had in a while. Lately, I have had to have my head in a much darker place. I have been working on book three in my paranormal dystopian series and it has been really taking its toll. The research into the occult and mysticism is overwhelming, so being outside walking around in the fresh air is just what I need.

Will, Jake, Antonia, and Mischief headed back to the house an hour ago after the little bundle of energy passed out in her father's arms. This allows Sophia and I to walk around and talk without fear of interruption.

"So what do you say?" Sophia stops in front of the palm reader's tent. A sign hangs on the front saying "Mistress Evangeline" in ornate lettering.

"You cannot be serious."

"Come on. It will be fun."

"Fine, but I don't like it."

We enter the tent to find a woman in a complete gypsy garb. It takes a minute for my eyes adjust to the candlelight, but there is a crystal ball, and a stack of tarot cards on the table in front of the fortuneteller.

"Enter. Enter." The woman gestures from her table. "Please sit."

Sitting down in front of the woman, I can't help but think that I know this woman. Her voice mimics the one that I hear every so often in my head. *Where do I know her from?*

"You." Mistress Evangeline points to Sophia. "Your hand."

After putting a five-dollar bill in the jar, Sophia tentatively gives her hand to the woman.

"You are an artist by trade, but have more savvy than most. Yet I am seeing a veer in course. You will remain creative, but differently than in the past. Your friendship with a scribe will open new doors for you. This collaboration will give you more time with the ones you love." Thinking that she is finished, Sophia begins to pull her hand away until the woman grabs it tighter. "Do not turn away the gift that has been given to you. It will be a struggle, but you will soon have a full home and heart. Tears have come and anger has exploded, but laughter and happiness will win out in the end."

"Holy shit." Sophia's brow is furrowed as if she knows exactly what this woman is talking about.

"Now you." Mistress Evangeline shifts in her seat to face me. She doesn't even wait for the money before she grabs both of my hands. Then she smiles as her eyes flicker with a hint of gold. "Ahh... I hoped we would meet again."

"Do I—"

"Shhh... There was once flames and uncertain ground that sent you down a path far different than the one you are on today. Decisions out of your control forced your hand, but you made the choice to save yourself and become who you are supposed to be. The voices have spoken to you in various forms and will continue to do so for many years to come. Listen to them and continue to tell their stories. You have chosen your anchor and he will serve you well. Do not question the bond that you share, because though it was quick, it was just fate showing you that you were on the right journey. Together there will be much love in your lives, but I caution you not to try to fit into a mold. The normal order of things may not be what is. Jump into the unknown and have faith. You have found your forever." She pulled away.

As we get up to leave, she stands and says, "Camilla."

"How do you—"

"Your fortune has been read once before. Since then, you have created your own fate. Know that the power is inside of you to get through whatever obstacles that lay in front of you. Shit happens. It is how you deal with it that makes you stronger and creates the path to who you are supposed to be."

Acknowledgments

FIRST AND FOREMOST, I HAVE TO THANK MY MOM. I am not an easy person to deal with and through this whole process she has been extremely supportive. She deserves all the thanks in the world and possible an endless supply of wine. Though, I am grateful for having two parents that encouraged me to follow my passions in life, my mother has shown me what real strength is over the last ten years.

This book has been quite the undertaking and there are a bunch of other people I need to express my gratitude toward. To Kiki, Ruth, and everyone over at The Next Step PR, you are amazing. I am happy to have you on my team for this book and hopefully many more down the road. To Nadine at A Whisper to A Dream and Shelly at Small Edits, you ladies rock. Thank you so much for your feedback with this book. To Jessa I appreciate you reading about Cami not once, but twice.

I also have to thank Nina Lane and Codi Gary. I don't think that I have ever valued relationships more that with the two of you. You let me pick your brains and have been excited for me since I first told each of you I was writing this.

For all the bloggers and reviewers who have decided to take a chance on this book, I thank you from the bottom of my heart. A special thanks to Katrina, Kat, Kathy, Kimberly, and Samien for all of your support. I am so happy that we were all introduced to each other through the XOXperts.

Finally, I have to thank the readers of this book. This has been a truly amazing experience for me and I hope that you like Cami and her friends as much as I do.

About the Author

VICTORIA COLOTTA IS AN ARTIST, AUTHOR, AND award-winning graphic designer for her work at VMC Art & Design. With a BFA from the School of Visual Arts in NYC and a voracious need to be reading, Victoria managed to merge the two loves in her life…art and books. As an artist, she is always exploring new ways to create and share her artwork. As an author, her goal is to push herself to explore all the aspects of her characters and their stories no matter where they may lead her.

Spending most of her day in her studio with her crazy dog Lizzy, Victoria loves to cook, bake, and read in her free time. She also enjoys talking with other readers, fellow book nerds, coffee addicts, authors, and artists on social media.

Stay Connected
with Victoria on...

Instagram.com/vcolotta

Facebook.com/vcolotta

Twitter.com/vcolotta

Goodreads.com/vcolotta

Sign up for Victoria Colotta's Newsletter!
https://tinyurl.com/vcolottanewsletter

You can also enjoy all things Art, Books, & Coffee at
www.artbookscoffee.com, on Instagram @artbookscoffee,
and in the Art, Books, & Coffee Facebook Group
(Facebook.com/groups/ArtBooksCoffee).

If you enter into a world of books,
you will always be an adventure.

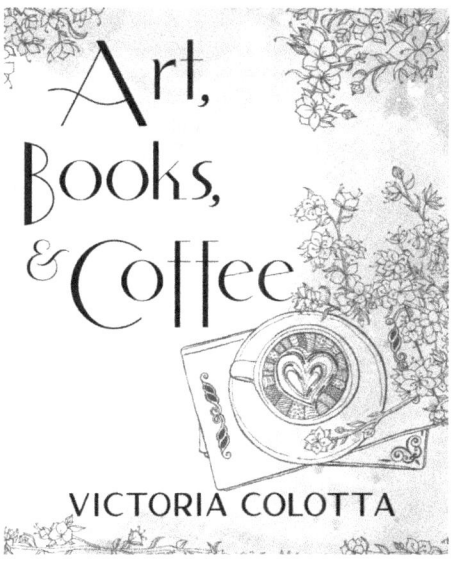

Inspired by the three passions in her life, artist and author Victoria Colotta has created her first solo coloring book—ART, BOOKS, & COFFEE. It is a collection of carefully curated hand-drawn illustrations using the books of some of today's bestselling authors as well as photographs from the top bookstagrammers.

As you color your way through the book, you will be able to sit in a New York City cafe, enter into a fairyland, and enjoy some wonderfully bookish renderings. This coloring book is the perfect way to unwind in a world of art, books, and coffee.

Find out more on
https://www.vcolotta.com/art-books-coffee

COINS
FOR THE
FERRYMAN

A novel by Leone Sperling

© Leone Sperling 1981, 2014

Leone Sperling asserts the moral right to be identified as the author of 'Coins for the Ferryman'.

First published 1981 by Pan Books (Australia) Pty Limited.

This edition published by Cilento Publishing, Sydney Australia.

Typeset and cover design by Green Avenue Design.

ISBN: 978-0-9925601-6-4